By
Kimberly Kirby

ISBN-13: 978-0-578-71973-3

DEDICATION

To everyone who has spoken encouraging words, offered kind advice or just a listening ear, you have my eternal love.

Thank you.

ACKNOWLEDGMENTS

For my husband, Rod, who has worked tirelessly to make sure my dreams come true, I love you more than you can imagine.

Thank you.

CHAPTER ONE

Virginia Johnson makes her way off of the bus after a long trip across town.

"Night, Ms. Virginia." Fred, the driver waves as Virginia limps down the steps holding the bus rail.

"I'll see ya tomorrow, Fred." Virginia smiles a sweet grin as she limps away.

Virginia Johnson has been riding the same bus route driven by Fred Thompson for fifteen years, ever since she started working in the school cafeteria at Kimbrough Elementary School. She is the head cook in the cafeteria and loves her job. She looks forward to going to work every morning to feed her "babies," as she calls them.

Virginia begins the ten-minute walk to her house. She spots the convenience store on the corner and pops in to play her numbers. She's been playing the lotto for ten years. Ever since the night she had a dream she won 4 million dollars.

In the dream, Virginia ran up and down the street praising God and dancing a two-step. She knows that on her bad knee she'd never be able to run like she did in the dream if she won, but that won't stop her from playing her numbers.

"Heyyyy, Ms. Virginia!" Dante, the store clerk, shouts as she pushes through the glass door. "Heyyyy, back at ya," Virginia shouts back as she makes her way in. "How ya mama doin?" "She good. She babysittin my lil girl tonight." Dante flashes a proud smile.

"Tell that baby I'm still waiting on her to come see me." Virginia grabs her favorite barbecue pork rinds and tosses them onto the counter.

"I'll bring her by, Ms. V." Dante scans the pork rinds and reaches above his head to pull down a lotto ticket.

"You playin yo numbers today, Ms. V?" He waves the ticket toward her.

"Boy, ain't no sense in actin brand new. Gimme that ticket and toss in one of those scratchers too." Virginia points to the scratch-off tickets and chuckles.

Dante used to be one of her babies at Kimbrough Elementary. She has watched him grow from a skinny little chocolate boy, scared of his own shadow, into a grown man with a child of his own.

Virginia pays for her goods and heads out of the door and tries her best to make her way home before dark. She loves her neighborhood, but over the years, she's had to watch it deteriorate.

She recalls how proud she was to buy a house in this area with her husband thirty years ago. It used to be full of proud black homeowners that took pride in watching out for one another. Now, you're lucky to make it to your car without getting robbed at night.

She grabs the railing and climbs the three steps in front of her house. Her cell phone vibrates in her pocket. She opens the door of her home and shuts the door behind her, locking it with the deadbolt. She collapses in her favorite chair and digs her phone out of her
pocket. She already knows who it is without looking at the screen.

"Girl, I can't even get in the house without you callin me." Virginia huffs as she catches her breath.

"Well, Well, hello to you too." Virginia's oldest daughter, Rita chuckles. She knew her mother would be aggravated by the call.

"Rita May, I can take care of myself. I do not need you checking up on me every day." Virginia scolds her daughter.

"I know, Ma. I told you, it's not for you. This is for my peace of mind. If you insist on walking home from the bus stop, then you have to deal with me calling you every day." Rita answers in a stern, loving voice.

"Baby girl, I have been taking care of myself since before you were born. I don't need no help. But thank you for checking on me, baby."

"Ma, if you just let me get you a car, I wouldn't feel the need to call you so often," Rita says hoping her mom will finally give in.

"Rita May, I already told you, I'm not takin no car from you. You don't take care of me. I am your mother. I take care of you."

Virginia shakes her finger as if Rita can see her.

Rita is a successful doctor. She worked hard to put herself through school. She knew her parents couldn't afford to send her through college. Virginia has always been proud of her daughter but can't bring herself to accept any help from her, although she needs it desperately. Her bills have piled up since her husband passed away 10 years ago. Recently the pain in her knee has been getting worse. Her doctor thinks she needs a knee replacement, but Virginia won't consider it as long as she can still take the pain.

"Alright Ma. Well, call me later," Rita says.

"Ok, baby, bye bye." Virginia presses "End" on her phone and places it on the table beside her.

She hears a rummaging noise coming from the back of the house. She grabs her phone instinctively. Just then, she sees a thin figure coming out of the dimly lit hallway.

"Hey ma," a weak voice says shakily.

"Sydney?" Virginia stands up and flicks on the light. "Hey, baby," she says.

Virginia's youngest daughter, Sydney emerges from the shadows. She walks across the room and hugs her mother. Virginia winces as the smell of her daughter's strong body odor overwhelms her.

She kisses Sydney on the cheek and puts her hands around her daughter's waist. Virginia fights back her tears.

"Well, girl, you are thinner than a blade of grass. When did you get here?" Virginia forces a smile.

"A couple hours ago. I missed you, Ma!" Sydney wraps her arms around her mother again. Virginia holds her breath as her daughter hugs her.

"It's been a long time, baby girl. Where you been staying?" Virginia motions for Sydney to sit on the couch.

"Here and there, mostly with some friends." Sydney's eyes shift from side to side as she scratches her neck.

Virginia has known about her daughter's drug problem for a while now. For some reason, Sydney still thinks she's hiding it from her mother. It all started during Sydney's sophomore year at the University of Memphis. She fell head over heels for a dealer that hung out and sold to kids on campus, Reggie. She tried it once and that was that. Instead of going back to school for her junior year, Sydney dropped out. Reggie lost interest in her once she got addicted, and with him gone, Sydney did anything she could to get her next high. Anything.

"I made a pot of spaghetti last night. You stayin for dinner?" Virginia smiles.

"As a matter of fact, why don't you stay the night with me, baby? I still have some of your clothes here. You go take a shower and put some fresh clothes on. I'll get dinner ready." Virginia grabs her daughter's hand and squeezes.

Sydney is too weak to deny that she could use a safe place to sleep and a good meal. She heads off to the bathroom.

As soon as she hears the bathroom door close Virginia's tears flow. She wipes her face and grabs her chest to calm herself. She takes a deep breath and heads into the kitchen to heat up dinner.

Half an hour later, Sydney emerges from the bathroom. She wears an old t-shirt from her high school days and jeans that used to fit her snugly in college but are now hanging off her hips.

"Come on and get you a plate, baby." Virginia beckons from the kitchen as she pulls hot garlic bread from the oven.

Sydney is still holding the soiled clothes she was wearing before her shower.

"Go put those on top of the washer, baby, I'll wash all that for you." Virginia points toward the laundry room.

After putting her clothes away, Sydney makes her way into the kitchen. She notices the table is set for four.

"You expecting company, Ma?" Sydney looks confused.

"Now, don't get mad. I called Rita and Jack. It's been so long since I had all kids here for dinner. Look, just don't leave." Virginia's eyes beg.

Sydney plops down in a chair at the dining room table. She props her head up with her hand. Virginia sits down next to her.
"I know you and your sister don't get along, but you're still family. She loves you. If she seems a little judgmental...it's just because she wants what's best for you."

Sydney sits up straight.

"She doesn't want what's best for me, Ma. She thinks she's better than me. She is embarrassed by me and she doesn't want me in her family."

A quick knock on the door is followed by the jingle of keys as the front door opens. "Ma, you ok?" Rita yells through the house as she barges in. Rita is dressed fabulously as usual. The woman doesn't know the meaning of the word casual.

She neatly places her ten-thousand-dollar alligator skin Birkin bag on the sofa. It's tan and perfectly matches her heels and the tan stripe outlining her form-fitting skirt.

"I'm fine, baby, come on in."

Virginia limps over to Rita and gives her a tight hug. Rita looks confused.

"Momma, you told me to come over because you weren't feeling well. I dropped everything and rushed over here. Are you ok?"

Sydney walks out of the kitchen and leans against the door frame.

"Hey sis," she gives a weak smile.

Rita's jaw drops as she eyes the sister she hasn't laid eyes on in two years. She's shocked to see that somehow her sister is thinner than she was two years ago.

Sydney's once chubby cheeks are sunken in and her thick, dark hair is dirty and matted.

"Sydney?" Rita says in disbelief. She looks over at her mother. Virginia grabs Rita and pulls her over to Sydney.

"Your sister dropped in to surprise me today, Rita. I'm sorry I lied to you, but I just needed to see all my kids under one roof."

Jack knocks as he pops his head in the front door.

"There's my handsome son!" Virginia rushes over to Jack. She gives him a long hug.

Jack grabs his mom and spins her around.

"What's up, Ma? You lookin good, girl!" Jack laughs as he pulls her in for another hug.

Jack is tall, dark and handsome. Virginia always said he's the spitting image of his father. His dad always drew attention from the ladies and Jack is no different.

"Aw, my baby boy." Virginia smiles and pulls her son into the living room. "What's goin on, Ri Ri?" Jack gives his sister an up nod.

"Sydney?" Jack runs over and wraps his arms around his baby sister. "Jack-Jack!" Sydney squeals as she jumps on her big brother.

Virginia places her hand over her heart and smiles.

"How long has it been since all of my babies were in the same room?" She smiles with tears in her eyes.

"Let's go eat!" Virginia ushers them all into the kitchen. Sydney, Jack and Rita sit down at the table as Virginia fixes plates.

"Let me help you, Ma." Jack hops up and helps his mother. Rita leans back in her chair with her arms folded.

"So, Sydney, where you been, girl? What made you decide to show up all of a sudden?" "I missed my mother. I wanted to make sure she was alright," Sydney answers.

"And I guess it took two years for that, huh? It took two years for you to miss your mother?" Rita chuckles.

"It hasn't been two years since I've seen mom! It's been two years since I've seen you, bitch!" Sydney leans forward in her chair, glaring at her sister across the table.

Rita smirks. "Are you sure you came back because you missed her? Or did you come back to steal money out of her purse again? Or maybe to steal her jewelry this time?"

Virginia sets a plate of food down in front of Rita. She gives her a hard stare. "We not doin that tonight, Rita. Shut up and eat," she whispers in Rita's ear.

Jack hands a plate to Sydney and pats her on the back. Sydney grabs his hand and smiles at him.

Virginia seats herself at the head of the table. She reaches to her left and grabs Rita's hand, then grabs Sydney's hand on her right.

The two girls grab hands with Jack. They all bow their heads as Virginia covers them in prayer and blesses the food.

A week later, Virginia is making her way off the bus again. She waves goodbye to Fred.

"Take it easy, Virginia," Fred shouts as he closes the bus door.

She shuffles across the parking lot and shoves open the door of her favorite corner store. "How you doin, Ms. V!" Dante waves as he tosses his dreadlocks over his shoulder.

"I'm good, baby! How you doin?" Virginia says as she grabs her pork rinds and tosses them onto the counter. She likes to eat them in bed while she watches her shows at night.

Dante's eyes drop as she approaches the counter. He fidgets awkwardly. "Ms. V, um...I got to tell you something."

Virginia senses his tone is serious. "What's wrong, baby?" she asks.

"Your daughter, uh, Sydney, right? She been hanging out behind the store all day." Dante rings up the pork rinds and tosses them into a bag.

"Whatchu mean, hanging behind the store?" Virginia hands him two dollars for her snack.

"Back behind the dumpster back there." Dante motions with his head. He's too embarrassed to make eye contact with her.

Virginia feels chills down her spine. She spots the back door and stomps over to it. She peers out of the window and sees Sydney leaning against a man's car. Sydney grabs the man's belt and pulls him close to her. The man pulls cash out of his wallet and begins counting it out for her.

Virginia gasps as her stomach sinks.

"I ain't call the cops or nothin, Ms. V. My manager told me to, but I ain't do it." Dante stuffs his hands in his pockets to stop himself from fidgeting.

Virginia can hear him speak, but she can't look at him. She can't take her eyes off of her daughter.

Sydney kisses the stranger. He opens the back door of his car. Sydney climbs in and takes off her shirt as the man climbs in with her.

Virginia feels her blood boil. She flings open the back door and takes off toward the car. She finds herself standing next to the car watching Sydney unbuckle the man's belt, her bare breasts exposed. She unzips his pants and leans in toward his crotch.

Virginia yanks open the car door and grabs her daughter by the hair. She drags a topless Sydney backward out of the car. Sydney screams as she hits the concrete.

Sydney squints as the sun glares in her eyes. She blinks as her eyes finally focus on her mother's face.

Virginia is staring down at her in horror and disgust, her eyes wet with tears. "Getcho ass up!" she screams.

Sydney scrambles to her feet and clutches her naked breasts in her hands. As thin as she is, she has little to cover.

Virginia grabs her arm and pulls her daughter behind her as she marches home.

A crowd has formed like it always does whenever there's any type of commotion in the neighborhood.

People laugh and point as Sydney tries to keep her small chest covered with one hand as her mother's tight grip is locked around the other, pulling her down the street.

"Stop! Ma, let go!" Sydney shouts as she stumbles behind her mother.

Virginia has never walked home so fast. She shoves her key in the lock and throws her daughter into the house. Virginia's nostrils are flaring like an angry bull as she stares down her daughter.

Sydney collapses onto the couch.

"Ma, look...we were just talking. I wasn't...look I know what you think but..." Sydney stammers.

"In my neighborhood. You would do this to me in my neighborhood? Down the street from my house?" Virginia steps back and puts her hands on her hips.

"Ma, I know that guy. We used to date, and we just ran into each other at the store. I'm embarrassed you saw us making out in his car." Sydney lies.

"That's a damn lie and you know it!" Virginia shouts. "Ma, don't..." Sydney starts.

"Lie to me again!" Virginia dares her.

"Look, I know what you do out there. I don't want to know it, but I do. I know about all that poison you pumpin into your body and I know how you make ya money! I ain't nobody's fool!" Virginia screams.

Sydney looks at the floor, unable to look at her mother.

"You would bring that shit to my house?" Virginia shouts. "In front of my neighbors? My friends?"

Sydney sits up straight on the sofa. She's still clutching her naked chest.

"So, that's all you care about, huh ma? So, never mind the fact that your daughter is on drugs! Never mind she is hoein' herself out behind a corner store. You just don't want her to do it in your neighborhood, in front of your friends?" Sydney shouts back.

"I have done everything in my power to help you, lil girl!" Virginia yells.

"How do you help somebody who won't admit they got a problem? I offered to let you move back in with me. I tried to help you get back in school. I tried to get you to talk to the pastor down at the church! You won't let me help you! Every time I try, you just lie to me, or you run away!" Virginia sits down next to her.

"I have tried everything I could think of."

16

Virginia hands Sydney the throw blanket on the edge of the sofa so she can cover herself. Sydney wraps it around herself. She looks up at her mother.

"Yea, you tried everything except being honest with me in the first place. Maybe if you would have told me the truth, I never would have started with this shit, ma!"

Sydney's eyes stare daggers at her mother. "What are you talking about?" Virginia asks.

"Wrong question. You should be asking yourself, when did my daughter's issues start?" Sydney continues to stare intently.

Virginia feels a lump in her throat as she thinks back to ten years ago when her world was turned upside down after her husband died suddenly of a heart attack. Shortly after that, her daughter, Sydney began acting out, she started skipping school and being promiscuous with boys.

"I remember," Virginia answers softly.

"It was right after your father passed away." Virginia tries to reach for Sydney. "Nope." Sydney pulls away.

"It was actually a few months after he passed away while I was still crying and sad about missing my dad. Then my big sister, Rita, sits me down and tells me I need to stop crying because that man was her father, not mine.

Virginia's whole body goes numb. "What?" She shakes her head in disbelief. "Sydney, baby, listen..." Virginia reaches for her again.

"She also told me my father was some Mexican man. That's why I'm so light-skinned and the rest of my family is dark. That's why my hair is curly, and nobody else's is." Sydney stares out into space as she recalls the conversation she had when she was eighteen years old.

"Sydney..." Virginia tries to speak.

"I don't want to hear any more lies! Is it true?" Sydney is shaking as she jumps to her feet and stands over her mother.

Virginia stands to her feet and places her hand on Sydney's shoulder.

"Yes, it is, baby," she cries as she finally admits the secret, she never wanted to tell her daughter.

"So, everyone knew this except me huh? You cheated on Daddy? I mean, the man I thought was my daddy. And you were never gonna tell me?"

Sydney stomps away from her mother and runs out of the front door, still wrapped in the blanket. She runs down the street, her face wet with tears.

Virginia feels her body shivering as she recalls the night of Sydney's conception.

She had gotten off the bus one night that seemed like any other. As she made her way into the corner store that night, she rushed to the bathroom to relieve herself after a long bus ride. As she was washing her hands, she freezes as she hears a loud bang. She turns off the water and listens to the bathroom door as quietly as she can. Her heart felt like it might pound through her chest. She remembers hearing men screaming at the cashier to hand over money. Virginia held her hands over her mouth to cover her breathing. She heard another loud bang, then the scream of the woman running the register that night.

She heard three taps on the bathroom door. Virginia froze. She hoped they would go away if she didn't answer. Three more taps on the door. This time they were more forceful, aggressive.

"I know you're in there, bitch," a Hispanic man's voice whispered and chuckled. "I saw you when you went in." He laughed again. Virginia didn't answer. She slowly backed away from the door.

She prays silently, the faces of her husband and two kids running through her mind.

"I'll make a deal with you," he says.

"You open the door; I don't kill you." He chuckles.

"You don't open the door and I have to knock it down...then I'll knock it down and kill you. You never see your family again." He taps the gun on the door again.

"I got two babies," Virginia yells through the flimsy wooden door with the rusty lock.

She knows if he wanted to, he could have already kicked the door down. He's toying with her. Virginia feels her legs turn into noodles as she moves closer to the door.

"Please don't kill me," she cries as she leans on the door.

"I no going to kill you. I just want to talk to you," he says, as if he's being sincere.

Virginia unlocks the door and opens it. She stands face to face with a small Mexican man. He's barely taller than Virginia, who stands at 5 feet 2 inches. He wears a black leather jacket, white t-shirt and dark jeans. His head is shaved clean and he had a tattoo on his neck of two Spanish words that Virginia didn't understand, "Espíritu Maligno." She now knows the words meant "Evil Spirit."

Virginia remembers how she trembled as the man pushed his way into the bathroom. She remembers the look on his face as he made her undress and she stood naked in the disgusting gas station bathroom. She remembers how the dirty floor felt under her feet.

She can still hear the laughter of his friends as he pinned her against the sink and thrust himself inside her. She remembers the feeling of the cold steel as he shoved the barrel of his gun inside of her once he had finished. When he had had his fun, he looked her in the eyes and kissed her.

He pulled up his pants, winked and left. She sank to the ground, naked and cold. She shivered on the floor, but she couldn't move. The police found her twenty minutes later. Nine months later, Sydney was born.

Jack pulls up to Walgreens two blocks away from his mother's house. Sydney called him to come pick her up.

"Why are you wrapped in this blanket, girl?" Jack laughs as Sydney plops herself down in the passenger seat.

Jack notices the tears running down her cheeks. "You gon tell me what happened?" he asks.

Sydney tugs the blanket securely around her and ties it in a knot.

"How long have you known that I had a different father than you and Rita?" She sits up straight and eyes her brother.

Jack swallows hard and clears his throat. He's unable to look over at his sister. He taps the steering wheel nervously as he waits for traffic to clear so he can turn out of the parking lot.

"Yea, I've known for a while," Sydney blurts out. "Rita told me."

"Why the hell would she tell you that?" Jack rolls his eyes and shakes his head disapprovingly.

"Well, my sister might be evil, but at least she told me the truth. Charles wasn't my father, but I loved him. He was a great dad to me." Sydney wipes away a tear.

"He was a good man. I'm sorry I ain't tell you, Syd. I ain't know how." Jack reaches over and grabs his sister's hand as he speeds down the street.

"I know. I never blamed you for that. Mom should have told me. Rita only told me because she was always jealous of how close I was to Dad...I mean Charles." Sydney corrects herself.

"Aye, don't do that. He was your dad too. Maybe not biologically, but you know what I mean." Jack reassures her.

He pulls up in front of a beautiful two-story brick home and parks near the curb. Sydney looks around.

"Where are we?" she asks.

"This is my girl house, Sheila. I'm stayin wit her for a little while." Jack hops out of the car and runs around to open Sydney's door.

Sydney smirks at her brother as she gets out of the car.

"So, how long have you been with this one?" She smiles.

"Don't even start, Syd. She ain't like the other ones. I'm gon marry that girl," Jack says proudly.

Sydney laughs inside herself as she thinks of how easily her brother falls in love. It seems like every six months he finds the love of his life. He seems to always look for women who can take care of him. Jack has always had trouble standing on his own two feet and supporting himself. He's always living off of some woman that he swears he's in love with. Sydney thinks it has something to do with the way their mother spoiled him as a child.

Virginia used to make sure that Jack never lifted a finger around the house. Virginia and Charles were firm believers in woman's work and man's work. All Jack had to do was take out the trash and mow the lawn during the summer months. Virginia smothered that boy in love and attention and Jack ate it right up. It's Sydney's opinion that Jack has spent his entire adult life trying to find a woman to fill his mother's shoes.

"Well, I can't wait to meet her," Sydney lies.

"She ain't home. She's out of town for her job. She won't be back for a few days. You can stay here with me till she gets back," Jack offers.

Sydney breathes a sigh of relief as they walk to the front door. She really didn't feel like being around anyone new. She just needs time to clear her head. Jack unlocks the front door.

Sydney steps inside and gasps. It was beautiful. Hardwood floors, a fireplace, an open floor plan. There was an eat-in kitchen that opened up into the living room. It was obvious a single woman lived here. There was a hint of pink everywhere you looked, but it was tastefully done. The woman had sparkles everywhere, the mirrors, the bowls on her coffee table, the candle holders, everywhere.

"It's so glamorous. Your girl has good taste," Sydney says, still looking around.

"Yea, my baby has good taste. I told you she's the one. She's beautiful and smart. My girl is the whole package," Jack boasts.

"Well, I'm happy for you big bro." Sydney smiles.

"So, what does she do? This house is amazing," Sydney asks.

"She's a lawyer. I told you, beauty and brains...and booty, you know she gotta have a big booty." Jack laughs as he flops down onto the couch.

Sydney sits in a white recliner next to the couch. She admires a blush pink pillow covered in faux fur perfectly perched in the chair.

"So, are we gonna talk about you and ma?" Jack asks. Sydney takes a pause.

"I just wish I didn't know." Sydney shakes her head.

"I feel like I could have lived my whole life and I would have been so happy believing he was my dad. But now...it's like I can't get it out of my head, you know? Dad was my everything." She looks to Jack for understanding as the tears begin to flow.

"Is that why you started getting high?" Jack asks. Sydney looks embarrassed.

"Sorry, I ain't mean to..." Jack starts.

"Nah... it's cool. It was around that time. I mean once Rita told me, I felt like I lost a piece of myself. I was doing everything I could to get that piece back," Sydney answers.

"Syd, I know it's hard, but I think it's better that you know the truth," Jack responds. Sydney lets out a pained laugh.

"Yea, the truth. Which truth? That Charles wasn't my father or that my mother was a hoe that liked Mexican dudes?" Sydney shrugs

Jack gives her a confused look.

"A hoe?" Jack's face is as serious as Sydney has ever seen it.

"Look, I know you're her favorite child, but I'm pissed at her right now." Sydney rolls her eyes.

"Nah, Syd. You can be pissed all you want, but you ain't never calling her that again." Jack's jaw clenches tightly.

"She ruined my life. I would have never been on drugs if she hadn't cheated on Dad!" Sydney feels rage bubbling inside her.

Jack freezes.

"Cheated on Dad? Syd, Ma was raped."

Sydney blinks trying to make the words make sense. "What?" she asks.

"Ma got raped. She was at a gas station when it got robbed. Some dude wit a gun came in the bathroom and raped her." Jack's voice cracks as his words bring up the pain of seeing his mother's face that night, all those years ago.

"I didn't... I thought..." Sydney stammers.

"So, I guess Rita ain't tell you that part, huh?" Jack asks as he stands up.

"It's late, I'm bout to go lay down. You can sleep in the guest room upstairs." Jack heads down the hall to the master bedroom.

Sydney's mouth hangs open as she tries to process what she just heard. Her tongue feels like cotton and her breath is staggered. It feels like an elephant is sitting on her chest. A rush of emotions passes through her, but the most prevalent one, guilt.

She had been carrying this anger against her mother for ten years. Now she doesn't know if she should be mad at herself or Rita for not telling her the whole story.

Sydney reaches into her pocket and pulls out a small plastic bag. She opens it and sprinkles a white powder onto her fingertip and in one breath, quickly snorts it up her nose. She rubs what's left on her finger across her teeth and then licks it off. She shoves the bag back into her pocket.

A few days later, Jack is sitting at his desk, speaking to a customer over the phone. He adjusts the headset he's wearing and brings the microphone close to his mouth.

"Stop by my office when you get off that call." Jack's short, potbellied supervisor taps him on the shoulder as he waddles past Jack's desk.

Jack gives a nod of acknowledgment as he continues his call. Five minutes later, Jack taps on his supervisor, Glen's, office door.

"Come in, have a seat." Glen motions to Jack.

As Jack takes a seat on the opposite side of Glen's desk, there's a knock on the door. Glen motions for the woman outside to come in. Jack recognizes her as the human resources manager. He focuses his gaze on Glen as the chubby little man begins what sounds like a prepared speech.

"Jack, unfortunately, this will be your last day of employment at Smart Wireless. We have had several discussions regarding you not hitting your target numbers each month."

The human resources manager has seated herself next to Glen. She shuffles through the papers in a folder she brought with her.

"I thought you said I had until next month to bring my numbers up. Look, Glen, I have a lot going on in my personal life. I can't lose my job right now. I guarantee I can have my numbers up by next month." Jack searches Glen's face for compassion, but Glen won't make eye contact with him.

The human resources manager slides a white envelope across the desk to Jack. "I wish things could have worked out," she says awkwardly.

Jack snatches the envelope off of the desk. Glen continues on with his speech. Jack stands abruptly without letting him finish. He turns to walk out of the office but comes face to face with two security guards.

"This way, sir." The security guards motion Jack toward the lobby. Jack stomps past them to the lobby doors as they rush to keep up him.

Jack rushes outside. The security guards stop at the door and watch as Jack gets in his car and sits there with his hands on the steering wheel. Jack breathes in and out deeply as he clutches the steering wheel. He feels a lump in his throat as he tries to calm himself.

He looks up and notices the security guards are still watching him. He sees a few of his co- workers peering through a window at him.

Jack shoves his key in the ignition and speeds out of the parking lot.

Rita pulls into the reserved parking space in front of her and her husband Keith's office building. She checks her makeup in the rearview mirror. She pulls a tissue from her glove compartment and blots her lipstick.

A tap on her window startles her. Jack stoops down next to her car window so she can see his face. Rita rolls her eyes and unlocks her passenger side door to let him in. She's been ignoring her brother's calls for the last few weeks. She didn't need to answer the phone to know what he needed.

"I wouldn't have to show up at your job if you answer the phone," Jack says as he hops in the car and shuts the door.

"I figured you'd take the hint if I didn't answer," Rita says with a shrug.

"Don't do that, sis. You know I always come to you cause you're the only one I can come to," Jack says sincerely.

"Let me guess. You got fired, again?" Rita cocks her head to the side as she waits for a response.

"Rita, I swear, it wasn't my fault this time! I did everything I could." Jack lowers his head. Rita chuckles.

"Do you realize that you said the exact same thing last time? Jack, I cannot keep picking up the pieces every time you screw up! You are a grown-ass man; you should be able to keep a job longer than six months at a time!" Rita sighs in frustration.

"Why do you always have to make everyone around you feel like trash because they're not as successful as you are? We might not all be doctors like you and Keith, but we ain't failures. We work regular jobs, but that don't make you better than everybody else," Jack says in a low tone without looking at her.

"I never said you were a failure! And guess what, I have nothing to do with you working a so-called regular job." Rita gives him a light punch in the arm.

"I don't care what kind of job you have, as long you're not borrowing money from me every other month. I just want you to stand on your own feet. I offered you a job last year, but you refused to take it!" Rita looks at him, her lips pursed.

"I can't work for you. I don't want the whole family knowing my sister had to hire me cause I couldn't keep a job." Jack shakes his head.

"Look, I just need a few hundred till next month. You know I'm staying with Sheila now. I need to be able to give her some money every month. I don't want her to think I'm a bum. I'm gon ask her to marry me," Jack pleads.

"Marry you? You can't even take care of your damn self! You want a wife too? Then what? Kids? I will not be supporting you and your whole family! You need to get a damn job, Jack! And keep it this time!" Rita screams.

Jack eyes his sister and sucks his teeth.

"You know what, Rita? Don't worry about it." He nods his head as he angrily throws open her car door and gets out.

Virginia paces outside of a luxury downtown Memphis apartment complex. Rita lives on the eighth floor. Virginia runs her fingers through her hair as she breathes heavily to calm herself.

She straightens her clothes as she looks at herself in the large window. She hates coming to this building; the people are a little too snooty for her taste. Her daughter, Rita, however, loves it. She fits right in.

Virginia walks in calmly, trying to hide the slow-burning rage inside of her.

"Can I help you?" the chubby door man in his sixties cheerfully asks.

"I'm just going up to visit my daughter," Virginia replies. "You must be Rita's mother?" he asks.

Virginia is taken aback.

"Yes, how'd you know?" Virginia asks, she hadn't told her daughter she was coming.

"Ma'am, it's only five black families in this building. I know them all by name." He chuckles.

"Besides, you look like her," he adds as he extends his hand to shake hers.

Virginia gives a knowing smile.

"I guess you got a point there." She chuckles politely as she shakes his hand.

She feels her anger bubbling up again as she walks down the marble hallway and approaches the golden elevator doors. She presses the up button three times quickly as if it will make it come faster.

Once inside, the golden doors close on her leaving her alone in the tiny elevator. She stares at her reflection in doors. She sees a reflection of her younger, forty-year-old self. She feels the same brokenness she felt as she carried Sydney inside her. She feels the weight of the shame she carried as she told her husband she was pregnant with another man's child.

As the elevator doors open, Virginia stomps down the hallway to find door 807. She pounds on the door. She feels her heart beating as she bangs on the door again.

Rita snatches open the door. "Ma? What's going on?"
Virginia stares at her daughter, nostrils flaring.

"You told Sydney she wasn't your father's child?" she says breathing heavily as if she walked up the eight floors.

Rita looks left and right down the hall, making sure her neighbors don't see. She knows her mother isn't afraid to cause a scene.

"Ma, why don't you come in so we can..." Rita starts but is quickly interrupted. "Did you tell her that?" Virginia shouts at her daughter.

"After the only father she ever knew died, did you tell her he wasn't her father?" Virginia's voice gets louder.

"Ma, I... I was just trying to..." Rita starts.

Virginia raises her hand and slaps Rita across the face. She turns and makes her way back down the hallway.

Rita stands in the doorway, dazed and stiff as she holds her face. Rita steps back inside her condo and shuts the door behind her.

She walks slowly into the kitchen and grabs a half-empty bottle of vodka from the freezer. She opens it and takes a long drink as she turns up the bottle. She plops down onto a barstool. She takes another swig from the bottle.

"Your mama is crazy as hell. Tell her not to bring all that ghetto shit up in here," Keith, Rita's husband says walking into the kitchen.

"I could hear her yelling from the bathroom," he laughs.

"Don't talk about my mother like that." Rita looks at him sternly. Keith places a small, black leather case on the counter.

"I'm just saying... we're physicians with our own practice. It's hard enough to build a reputation as a black doctor. We don't need that type of shit ruining our reputation in this building," Keith explains as he unbuttons his shirt, takes it off and lays it across the counter.

He stands in the kitchen in a crisp white t-shirt, black slacks and dress shoes.

He reaches for the black case and unzips it. He pulls out a long rubber tube and wraps it around his arm and holds the other end firmly with his teeth. He takes a seat on a barstool across the counter from his wife. He pulls a needle out of the case and fills it with clear liquid from a small glass bottle.

"Do you really have to do that right now, aren't you on call tonight?" Rita shakes her head disapprovingly as she downs more vodka.

Keith pushes the needle delicately into his arm and squeezes the drug into his veins.

"I thought you said you were only going to use the fentanyl patches. How are people going to feel about being treated by a prestigious black doctor with track marks in his arms?" Rita asks mockingly.

"It's harder to get the patches, Rita. This is just temporary until I can get more of the patches." Keith pulls the needle out of his arm and puts it back in his case. He takes the tube off his arm.

"Keith, you promised me you were going to try to slow this down. I can't be married to a damn junkie." Rita jumps up and stomps over to the freezer, opens it and tosses the vodka on the top shelf.

"You keep talking about how you want kids. I'm not bringing kids into this shit." Rita says as she marches past Keith.

Keith grabs her arm and yanks her violently back toward him. He stands up and pushes her against the counter and pins her there.

"You have been doing this to me for the past five years, sweetheart. When do you think you'll be ready to have my child? How much longer do I have to listen to my mother bitch about grandchildren?" Keith asks in a low tone.

Rita swallows hard as her heart pounds in her chest.

"Baby, I'm just saying...I don't think you want our kids seeing their dad shooting up around the house," Rita says as sweetly as she can.

"I just think it's better if we wait until we can get you past this, don't you?" She puts her hands softly on his face.

Keith slaps her hands down and grabs Rita by her throat. She gasps for air as his fist closes tightly around her neck.

"Do you think I'm fucking stupid?" He breathes in her face.

"You think I'm dumb enough to be doing this shit in front of my kids? You know me better than that." Keith chuckles as he releases her neck slowly and strokes her cheek.

"Now, you promised me that we would start trying this year." Keith grabs his shirt off of the counter and slips it on. He buttons it as he stares her down.

"We are going to start trying next month. I'm done waiting."

Keith tucks his shirt in. He leans over and kisses his wife on the cheek before walking out of the apartment.

Sydney has been staying with Jack for the past two nights. She's been too embarrassed to go back to her mother's house and apologize. She passed out on the plush couch in Jack's girlfriend's living room last night and was too tired to get up and move to the guest bedroom upstairs.

Sydney suddenly feels someone standing over her. She slowly opens her eyes and blinks to focus on the woman standing next to the couch, hands planted firmly on her hips with a look of disgust on her face.

The brown-skinned woman wears a tailored light grey blazer with a pink camisole and matching light grey capri pants and high heels.

"What the hell are you doing in my house?" the woman asks, hands still on her hips. She kicks off her heels one at a time and unbuttons her blazer.

"So, not only did he bring a bitch in my house, he let her spend the night? In my house?" The woman screams, mostly talking to herself as she paces back and forth.

Jack stumbles into the living room in his boxer briefs with no shirt. He's still half asleep.

"Hey, baby, I thought you weren't going to be back until tomorrow," Jack says as he wipes his face with his hands.

"Oh, you thought you'd have more time to get this raggedy bitch out of my house, huh? Seriously Jack? This ho looks dirty!" Sheila charges over to him and gets in his face.

"Sheila, baby, calm down. This is..." Jack starts but is quickly cut off.

"I let your black ass move into my house and the first time I have to go out of town you do this?" Sheila furiously swings at him as Jack tries to restrain her.

Sydney folds her arms as she sits cross-legged on the sofa. She smirks at her brother.

"Baby! Listen to me! This is my sister! This is Sydney!" Jack yells as he pins her arms to her side to stop her from hitting him.

Sheila stops and thinks for a moment as she glances back at Sydney who is fighting to hide how amused she is.

"Remember before you left, I told you she was back in town? She was staying with my mom, but they got into it. I told her she could crash here for a few days while you were out of town. I'm sorry, baby, I should have told you about it." Jack frees her arms cautiously.

Sheila folds her arms across her chest suspiciously.

"So, this is your... sister?" she asks as if she's still not completely convinced.

"Baby, why else would she be sleeping out here on the couch?"

Jack grabs his wallet off of the counter and pulls out a picture of him, Rita and Sydney when they were kids. Sheila grabs the picture and eyes it.

"See, baby, she still looks the same. Her head was just as big back then as it is now."

Jack lets out a nervous laugh.

Sydney stands up and walks over to Sheila and gives her a sideways hug.

"Don't worry about it, girl, I've been called worse than a raggedy bitch." Sydney laughs.

Sheila gives an embarrassed smile.

A few days later, Sydney stands on her mother's front porch. She's about to knock on the door but quickly decides she's not ready to face her. Sydney turns and walks away.

The door flings open.

"You might as well come on in. I figured you'd be back," Virginia says as she holds the door open. She nods for Sydney to come in.

Sydney slowly moves into the house.

"Jack called and told me you were at his place. He didn't want me to worry about you." Virginia motions for Sydney to sit down.

Sydney seats herself on the dark red sofa with flower print and fringe along the edges. She twists the fringe between her fingers as she struggles to come up with the right words to say to her mother.

"Now, just let me say something before you start, baby," Virginia says as she takes a deep breath and sits down next to her daughter.

"You're right...I know you're right. I should have told you about your dad. I... I just didn't know how to tell you that Charles wasn't your dad without telling you about your real father." Virginia has tears filling her eyes as she speaks.

Sydney grabs her mother's hand.

"No, I'm sorry, Ma. I didn't know what happened to you." She wipes the tears now pouring from her mother's eyes.

"I never knew that he... he raped you." Sydney cries as she moves toward her mother.

She puts her head in Virginia's lap as she weeps. Virginia strokes her daughter's soft curly hair.

"I still should have told you. But I never wanted you to feel like I didn't want you." Virginia wipes Sydney's tears and forces her to sit up.

Virginia's voice shakes as she speaks.

"When I found out I was pregnant, I was already about twelve weeks along. I had been in such a fog since it happened, I never noticed any of the signs." Virginia turns to face Sydney.

"When the doctor told me I was pregnant, I knew it was by the man that raped me. It couldn't have been Charles because I hadn't let him touch me since it happened. Before that, we hadn't had sex for at least two weeks," Virginia explains.

"Why didn't you have an abortion?" Sydney asks, afraid of the answer.

"Because you were a part of me. I couldn't explain it, but I just couldn't do it. Believe me, I thought about it. I even went to the clinic, twice. I was terrified, but I knew you were still part of me. You felt like mine." Virginia squeezes Sydney's hand.

"I guess I didn't tell you because I didn't want you to feel like you weren't wanted. I didn't plan to have you, but I did choose to have you." Virginia smiles through her tears.

Sydney hugs her mother.

"Thank you for choosing me," she says as she squeezes her mother as tight as she can.

CHAPTER TWO

Two months later, Sydney feels as if she's floating as she stands outside of the YMCA. She spots her brother's car and jumps up and down as she flags him down.

"Thanks for picking me up," she says happily as she hops in the passenger seat.

"No prob, Syd. How was the meeting?" Jack asks.

Sydney pulls out a small bronze coin.

"I got my first 30-day chip today." Sydney smiles proudly. Jack grabs his sister and hugs her tightly.

"I'm proud of you, girl!" Jack says as he puts the car in drive and pulls out of the parking lot. "Thank you. It's a lot of work, but I'm doing it." Sydney smiles.

"Ma told me to ask you to stay for dinner once you drop me off. Can you stay?" Sydney asks.

"You know I'm always down to eat." Jack laughs as he speeds down the street. Twenty minutes later, the two pull up in front of their mother's house.

"Is that Rita's car?" Sydney asks as she spots the black Mercedes in the driveway.

"Yep, I guess she finally coming back around, huh? You know Ma slapped the shit out of her when she found out about her telling you about Dad." Jack chuckles to himself.

"You lyin?!" Sydney says, shocked.

"Nope, Ma told me bout it." Jack smirks.

Just then, they see Rita's car door open as she steps out and heads toward the front door.

"This is bout to be hilarious!" Jack lets out a roar of laughter as he unbuckles his seat belt.

"Ugh, I really don't want to deal with her tonight. I just wanted to celebrate my 30-day chip and eat some good food." Sydney rolls her eyes.

"Just think of it as entertainment for your 30-day sober party." Jack smiles. "Come on, let's go."

"What up, Rita?" Jack yells as he jogs up to the front door where Rita has just rung the doorbell.

"Hey Jack, hey Syd," Rita answers, as if annoyed by their presence. Virginia opens the front door and looks Rita up and down.

"Ma, you wouldn't answer your phone or respond to my texts. I had to come over," Rita says.

"Well, ya'll come on in. I got food on the stove." Virginia flings open the door and heads off into the kitchen.

Rita follows her as Jack and Sydney sit quietly in the living room, trying to pretend they aren't listening. Virginia bends over and takes a pan of baked chicken out of the oven.

Rita stands near the kitchen door, watching. She sees Virginia limping around as she moves about the kitchen.

"Ma, let me help you. Why don't you sit down and let me finish up?" Rita walks over to her mother and tries to take a stack of plates out of her hands.

"I don't need your damn help!" Virginia snatches the plates away from her daughter.

She limps over to the kitchen table and slams them down on the old wooden table. Rita freezes. She stands there a second to collect herself.

"I'm sorry, Ma," she says.

Virginia sits herself in a chair at the kitchen table and rubs her knee.

"Did you hear me, Ma? I said I'm sorry?" Rita says, her voice trembling.

"You were old enough. You knew exactly what happened to me. But for some reason, when you told your sister about it, you left out the most important part of the story."

Virginia stares at Rita whose feet seemed glued to the kitchen floor.

"I've been thinking about it for weeks now. You did that on purpose. That was hateful." Virginia stares brokenheartedly at her daughter.

Rita walks over and sits down beside her mother. "It was. I know that now." Rita nods her head.

"I guess I always felt that you and Dad did so much to make sure she felt loved that I always ended up feeling like ya'll didn't care about me." Rita wipes away a tear.

"And then when Dad died, everyone gathered around her. Everyone wanted to make sure she was ok because she was the baby. They made sure Jack was ok because he was the only boy. But I felt like no one cared if I was ok. I was hurting too!" Rita holds her chest as she tries to control her breathing.

"No one checked on me. I was the oldest. I was always the one who had to hold it together and be an example for them. I never got to express how I was feeling, and I felt like no one would have cared if I tried to." Rita fights to push the words out.

Virginia looks at her.

"I never knew you felt like that. I guess I always thought of you as the strongest. You were the one that helped me with the rest of them. You were always so headstrong. You never liked to talk about how you felt about anything," Virginia explains.

"When your father passed, my life was a blur for at least six months. All I remember is Sydney and Jack cuddling up in my bed with me. They cried with me. They always wanted to talk about him, see pictures and hear stories about him. I stayed in that fog for months. I don't remember much else." Virginia reaches up and touches Rita's face.

"But I do remember your strength. You cooked dinner. You took the kids back and forth to school. I remember feeling so thankful for your strength. Especially at a time when I didn't have it." Virginia smiles at her.

"I should have checked in on you more, baby. I should have asked how you felt more." Virginia grabs Rita's hand.

"I wasn't that strong, ma. I would cry almost every night. I just felt like no one cared. Then one day I see Sydney crying, again. I just snapped. I felt like everything was about her. I was just so tired of her always crying." Rita looks off, staring at the wall.

"Me and Dad were close before you had her. I was his little girl. Once she came along, he chose her." Rita looks back at her mother.

"I snapped." Rita looks down at the floor.

"I remember how close you and Dad were. Ya'll did everything together. But I don't think he ever chose her over you. I think once she came along, you didn't like sharing him with her." Virginia corrects her.

"I'm always gonna love you, baby. But what you did to your sister... that was wrong." Virginia stands and walks over to a big pot on the stove and begins to stir it.

"I know. I'm sorry. How can I make it right, Ma?" Rita walks over to her mom.

"You wanna get right with me, you need to get right with your sister." Virginia turns off the stove and walks out of the kitchen.

Rita takes a breath and taps her foot before walking into the living room.

"Syd, can I talk to you for a minute?" Rita asks humbly.

Sydney glares at her sister from her seat on the couch. "Why?"

Sydney rolls her eyes and slowly stands to her feet. "I need to talk to you about..." Rita starts.

"Yea, I heard what you told ma. I'm not interested." Sydney folds her arms.

"Not interested?" Rita steps back and places her hands on her hips.

"Not interested." Sydney repeats herself firmly as she looks her sister up and down.

"You have no idea what I've been through. For the last ten years, you have made me feel like my parents didn't want me. Like they were just stuck raising me because they didn't believe in abortion. You are the reason I spent the last six years of my life on drugs! I am not interested in a damn thing you have to say right now." Sydney's face is wet with tears as she speaks.

Rita can feel the rage bubbling up inside her.

"You see, that is why I could never stand your ass! You always blame your shit on other people! You can never just take responsibility for your choices! I didn't put the crack pipe in your hand, baby girl! You did that yourself!" Rita stomps over to the recliner in the corner of the room where her purse sits. She snatches it up and tosses it on her shoulder.

"I tried, ma. I'm done. I can't do this with her." Rita walks out of the front door slamming it behind her.

A few weeks later, Rita stands outside of her condo. She takes a deep breath before unlocking the door.

"So, where did you go after you left the office?" Keith asks as Rita walks in the door.

Rita had hoped that he'd be passed out by now. She's grown accustomed to his schedule since he started using about five years ago. Normally, as soon as he gets home, he throws back a few shots, shoots up and passes out on the couch around nine o'clock. He wakes up a few hours later to do it all again.

"Sorry, I needed to drive around. I had to clear my head. I had a long day," Rita says as she walks past Keith seated on the couch. She tosses her bag on the kitchen counter.

"Well, I'm sorry you had a long day, babe." Keith makes his way over to her.

"But baby, it's almost ten o'clock, I was worried about you." Keith stands in front of Rita and places his arm around her waist, pulling her towards him. He kisses her cheek softly.

Rita tries to hide that his touch now makes her cringe. She grabs his face and pulls it toward her, she kisses his forehead like she does every night.

"You wouldn't be avoiding me, would you, baby?" Keith works his hands down his wife's body. He caresses her curves and looks into her eyes.

"Why would I be avoiding you?" Rita gives an unenthusiastic smile and tries to walk away from her husband.

Keith grasps her wrist tightly and yanks her back to him.

"I know you're ovulating this week, Rita." Keith glares at her.

"Did you think I forgot? You promised me that we would start trying this month. I've been keeping up with your cycle."

Rita tries to free herself of his grip.

"Baby, I wasn't avoiding you. I... I have the worst headache tonight, baby. How about we try tomorrow?" Rita cups his face with her hand. She leans in and kisses his cheek.

She turns and starts to walk away again.

Keith grabs her by the neck and slams her into the wall. A wedding picture of the pair falls from the wall. The glass frame shatters across the hardwood floor.

Keith's grip closes tightly around her neck.

"You promised me that we would start trying today." Keith's jaw clenches tightly as he pins her against the wall.

"Baby, I'm just not ready to be a mom. I think I just need a little time to focus on building up our practice." Rita eeks out the words as she puts her hand around Keith's hand as it squeezes around her throat. She struggles to fight the tears forming in her eyes.

"You've had five years! You're forty-three years old, sweetheart. You are not getting any younger." Keith's nostrils flare as he speaks.

"Listen to me! We are not ready!" Rita yells as she claws his hands off of her neck.

"I'm not doing this! We are not ready to bring a child into this relationship! Look at us, we can't even have a damn conversation without screaming at each other. I don't care how pissed off you get! Listen to me good, Keith. I'm not having a child in the middle of this shit!" Rita pushes away from Keith and walks to the bedroom and slams the door behind her and locks it.

Virginia pushes open the convenience store door and slowly makes her way inside.

"Hey, Mrs. V!" Dante yells from behind the counter. He flashes a bright smile, tosses his long dreadlocks over one shoulder and continues helping the customer in front of him.

"Hey, back at ya!" Virginia waves at him as she heads over to pick up a bag of barbecue pork rinds.

Virginia heads up to the counter and waits for Dante to finish up with his customer.

"Let me get one of them Mega Million tickets," the young man asks as he pulls a few more dollars from his wallet.

"I forgot that drawing is tonight," he says as Dante hands him a ticket.

The young man quickly marks his numbers on the ticket and passes it back to Dante. He nods at Virginia waiting patiently behind him as he heads out of the store.

"I already know you want that Powerball ticket, huh? How many you want?" Dante flashes his beautiful white teeth.

"You already know it. Don't act brand new." Virginia winks at him and chuckles as she tosses her pork rinds onto the counter.

"You need to get in on this Mega Million, Mrs. V. You know it's up to $65 million, right? The drawing is tonight." Dante points to the tickets.

"Nah, that ain't how I roll. I'll let Ya'll young folks jump from game to game chasing that big money. I just play my Powerball. Your odds are better if you stick with one game." Virginia nods and points her finger as if she's teaching him a scientific fact.

"Yea, but $65 million, Mrs. V? You seriously not even gon try?" Dante asks as he rings her up.

"I'll let you young folk have that one." Virginia brushes him off as she pays for her goods.

"Well, fine, this one will be on me." Dante smiles as he tears off a ticket and hands it to her. He fishes a few dollars out of his pocket to pay for the ticket.

"Boy, I bet you could bug a fly!" Virginia says as she snatches the ticket from him and marks random numbers on it without thinking.

Dante lets out a loud laugh as he rings up the ticket.

"You know I gotta look out for you, Mrs. V!" he says, laughing.

Virginia chuckles as she grabs her receipt and walks to the door.

"Tell your mom I said hi and kiss that baby of yours for me," Virginia says as she pushes the door open and leaves.

Later that night, Virginia is relaxed in her favorite recliner with her feet propped up. The chair used to be her husband's favorite before he passed away. Now that he's gone, Virginia always sits there. It makes her feel closer to him somehow.

Virginia snacks on pork rinds as she watches the news. She takes a sip of her homemade sweet tea.

She hears the news reporter talk about the lottery. Suddenly, she realizes she doesn't have the tickets in her hand. She hops up and rushes as fast as she can on her bad knee to her bedroom. She quickly rummages through her purse and fishes out the tickets. She can hear the numbers being called out in the living room. She hurries back to the television and stands in front of it reading her tickets.

The announcer has already called out all of the numbers and they are displayed at the bottom of the screen: 14 – 22 – 30 – 37 - 60 - 8.

Virginia's breathing is shallow as she blinks at the Mega Millions ticket Dante bought her. She feels her entire body tremble. She pants as she tries to catch her breath. She takes a few steps back and collapses in her chair right as she feels her legs give out.

She grabs the remote and pauses the television. Her mouth hangs open as her gaze goes from the TV back to the ticket, then back to the TV.

She reaches for her glass of iced tea and brings the glass to her mouth, but her hand is shaking so badly that she can't drink it. Just then, she hears Sydney's keys in the front door. The glass slips from her hand and smashes on the hardwood floor. Sydney rushes in the front door seeing her mother's shocked expression.

"Ma, what happened?" Sydney asks as she hurries over to Virginia.

"Ma, you ok?" Sydney asks as she grips her mother's face.

Virginia can't speak. She stares at Sydney in shock and tries to force the words out, but they won't come.

"Ma, what's wrong?" Sydney kicks the broken glass out of the way with her shoe. She gently slaps Virginia's face to make her speak.

Virginia hands Sydney the lottery ticket she has clutched in her fist.

"I... we... the..." Virginia tries hard to get the words out. She pants heavily and points to the television still paused on the winning numbers.

Sydney forces her eyes to focus on the ticket then follows Virginia's finger to the television. Sydney gasps and looks at her mother.

Two months later, Rita unlocks the front door of her mother's house. She walks in and finds Virginia writing in a spiral notebook.

"Ma, you're the only person I know that can win $65 million dollars and not spend a dime of it in two months," Rita says as she walks in and kisses her mother on the cheek.

Virginia flips the notebook closed.

"Technically, I didn't win $65 million, since I had to split it with the other two folks that won," Virginia responds.

Rita sits next to her mother on the sofa.

"Yes, yes, I know. But you still won $21 million, right?" Rita jokes.

"I have got to do right with this money, baby. I'm not spending nothing until I know exactly what I'm gone do with it." Virginia smiles as she grabs her notebook and flips through it.

"So, is that what you've been writing in this book? This is why you locked yourself in the house?" Rita reaches for the notebook.

Virginia pulls it away from her.

"My head is all jumbled. I keep daydreaming about spending it. But I don't wanna be like them other fools that win some money and five years later they broke again. I have to plan this out right." Virginia presses the notebook to her chest.

"Ma, you don't have to be perfect with this money. You're entitled to go a little crazy. I mean, yes you want to make sure you don't blow it all in five years. But Ma, I have watched you struggle my entire life. I just want to see you get to buy somethings for yourself for once," Rita explains.

"I will spend it. I just need more time to plan, baby." Virginia pats her daughter on the leg.

"Ma, you haven't even quit your job yet! You're still riding that damn bus every day! You won't even buy yourself a car. Ma, I think you're in shock. It's like you don't believe it's real yet." Rita grabs her mother's hand.

"I know it's real! I check my bank account every morning to make sure it's still there! This type of money has the ability to change your life. I don't know if I want a new life! Ya'll keep telling me to buy a new house and quit my job. I love my job! I love my house! I raised my babies in this house! I loved your father for twenty-seven years in this house." Virginia clutches her notebook and rocks side to side

45

"Ma, you don't have to sell the house. You can keep it and rent it out." Rita tries to comfort her mother.

"I don't want nobody else living in my house," Virginia says in a whisper.

"Ma, I'm just worried about you. Whether you realize it or not, you are a multi-millionaire now. It is not safe for you to be living in this neighborhood and riding the bus every day." Rita squeezes her mother's hand.

"Nobody knows I won. I claimed the money anonymously," Virginia replies.

"Ma, eventually people will figure it out. Word travels. Then folks will start targeting you. Come on, let's talk about your first purchase. Once you start to spend a little, you'll feel more comfortable." Rita nudges Virginia jokingly.

"I already know the first thing I'm doing with money, after I pay my tithes, of course. I'm giving Dante $5 million." Virginia smiles to herself.

"You're kidding, right? Ma, tell me that's a joke." Rita sits up straight.

"If it weren't for that boy, I never would have won. He bought me the ticket," Virginia answers firmly.

"So, give him his three dollars back! Ma, you can't give him $5 million dollars!" Rita pleads.

"My mind is made up. I don't want to hear it, Rita! If it weren't for him, I wouldn't have a dime," Virginia reminds her.

"Ok, how about you give him five thousand, ten thousand? Hell, I'd even be ok with giving him fifty thousand dollars, but you can't just..." Rita starts.

"Don't tell me what I can't do with my own money!" Virginia scolds.

Sydney's keys are heard in the front door. She walks in, eyes Rita and walks past her to get to Virginia.

"Hey Ma," she leans in and gives her mother a kiss on the cheek.

"You still planning, huh?"

"Yes ma'am," Virginia pats her notebook.

"Your sister came over to help me. You wanna sit down and help?" Virginia asks.

"No, Ya'll go ahead, ma. I'm sure she has plenty of ideas." Sydney rolls her eyes and heads back to her room.

Rita folds her arms and lets out an annoyed sigh.

"How much money would it take to fix you two? All I have ever wanted is to be able have all my kids in one room without them trying to kill each other." Virginia gets up and walks into the kitchen.

Three weeks later, Virginia stands outside of her bank. She's been planning long enough and she's ready to start spending her money.

"You ready to do this, Mrs. Johnson?" Victoria Adams asks as she approaches Virginia in the parking lot.

Victoria is an attorney Virginia called last week. Virginia takes a deep breath. "I'm ready. Is all the paperwork done?" she asks.

"All I need is your signature. Let's do it." Victoria smiles and ushers Virginia into the bank. Rita pulls a blood pressure pump off of her patient's arm.

"Well, you didn't lie, Mrs. Clark, your blood pressure has improved, and your cholesterol levels are heading in the right direction. Good work!" Rita gives Mrs. Clark a high five.

"I told you I had been working on it!" Mrs. Clark, a portly sixty-five-year-old black woman, chuckles.

"Now, I did give you a weight loss goal of ten pounds. You only lost four pounds. Have you been exercising?" Rita folds her arms and gives a sly smile.

"I ain't got time for no exercises. I got my church meetings and my grandbabies to keep me moving." Mrs. Clark folds her arms and returns Rita's sly smile.

"We have been over and over this, Mrs. Clark. It is very important for a woman your age to take care of herself. You need to eat well and lose some weight so you can be around to see those grandbabies grow up, ok?" Rita puts a hand on Mrs. Clark's shoulder.

"Dr. Powers?" Rita's receptionist, Trish, gives a quick knock and pops her head in the doorway.

"I am so sorry to interrupt. We have a situation in the next room."

Rita excuses herself and follows Trish to the next room. She stops in her tracks when she sees her husband shaking on the floor. He's foaming at the mouth; his eyes have rolled to the back of his head.

"I didn't know what to do, I didn't know what to do," Trish mumbles as she stares helplessly at Keith.

Rita rushes quickly to Keith and drops to her knees next to him.

"Go get my purse!" Rita screams to Trish as she pulls a penlight out of her pocket and checks his pupils.

She rolls a seizing Keith on to his side. Rita rips off her white coat, balls it up and places it under his head to cushion it. She grabs a tissue from a nearby tray and wipes his mouth.

Trish runs back into the room with Rita's purse and hands it to her.

"Stand back!" Rita shouts as she tries to hold Keith with one hand and dig through her bag with the other.

She fishes out a small white bottle and yanks off the cap with her teeth. She carefully hides the label with her hand as she gives Keith a quick spray in his nostril.

"Is he ok? Should I call 911?" Trish shouts.

Rita ignores her and continues to work on Keith. The seizing begins to slow down. She lays him flat on his back and gives him CPR. She pumps his chest and blows in his mouth.

"I'll call 911!" Trish yells and turns to run for the phone. "Don't call them!" Rita yells frantically.

"I mean, thank you. But I've got it. He's fine...see? He's coming out of it." Rita responds as calmly as she can.

Keith lies still on the floor. His eyes bounce around the room, trying to understand how he ended up on the floor.

"He's been having a few health issues. He doesn't like to talk about it. You know how men are. But he's ok. I'll monitor him here for a while. Mrs. Clark is finished next door. Can you show her out? And close that door behind you please," Rita asks.

As the door closes, Rita turns to Keith who's still disoriented. She holds the small white bottle up to his face to make sure he can see the bold writing on the label that reads: NARCAN.

"I can't keep doing this shit, Keith!" she whispers sternly.

She rolls off her knees onto her bottom as the emotion of what just happened catches up to her. She breaks down in tears as she grabs his hand.

"I can't do this anymore, Keith." Rita sobs.

Jack rushes around Sheila's home. He lights the candles he's placed along the stairway. He spreads rose petals on the floor leading from the front door to the living room where he has more candles and flowers all over the room.

He sees the headlights from Sheila's car shine through the window. He pulls his phone out of his pocket, turns the camera on and hits the record button. He props his phone up on the countertop and aims the lens toward the center of the living room.

Sheila opens the door and freezes as she sees Jack standing there in a black suit holding a bouquet of pink roses.

"Oh, my God," she whispers, her mouth hanging open.

"Welcome home, baby," Jack says walking over to her.

He grabs paperwork she has tucked under her arm and hands her the flowers. He takes her hand and leads her over to the sofa and ushers her to sit down.

"Jack, what are you doing?" Sheila has a shocked expression on her face.

"Baby, you are the most amazing woman I have ever met in my life. You have had my heart since the first time I saw you. You make me think about all the things I want out of life. I decided that I'm ready to start a real life. I'm ready to be happy. I'm ready to start a family...and I want you to be my wife." Jack smiles as a tear rolls down his cheek.

He reaches into his pocket and pulls out a small black box. Jack opens the box and drops down on one knee. He holds the box up to Sheila. The ring is a thin, simple gold band with a small diamond.

"Will you marry me?" Jack asks humbly.

"Baby...I... um. I would love to marry you. But..." Sheila stammers.

Jack jumps up and grabs her and squeezes her tightly. He kisses her passionately on the lips. Jack pulls the tiny ring out of the box and tries to put it on her finger.

"Baby, baby! Wait!" Sheila stops him.

"Sweetie I love you, and I love that you did all this for me. You are such a good man," she adds as she wraps her hands around his hands.

"Babe, I don't think we're ready to get married. We've never even talked about it!" Sheila squeezes his hands.

Jack takes his hands out of hers and slides a few inches away from her on the sofa.

"I know we didn't talk about it. But I just figured if we talked about it, you wouldn't be surprised when I proposed," Jack explains.

"I get that, sweetie. I do. But if we had talked about it, you would have known that I don't think we're ready. I mean, you would have known that...before we got to this point." Sheila puts her hand on his leg.

"Baby, this doesn't mean that I don't love you. But I've just been seeing you struggle for months now. You've been bouncing around from job to job. I mean, you haven't even found a new job yet since the last one." Sheila reaches for his hand, but he pulls it away.

"I'm looking for a job, you know that," Jack mumbles as he puts the ring back in the case.

"Yes, I know. But I think you seem to be just running from job to job trying to find yourself. Remember we talked about you going back to school? Whatever happened to that?" Sheila asks softly.

Jack fidgets with the ring box silently without looking at her.

"Jack, I would absolutely love to marry a sweet, kind, funny man like you. But I need my husband to not only be sweet, funny and kind. I need my husband to be stable. I need my husband to have goals and a plan. He needs to have some direction for his life."

Sheila slides up close to him and grabs his hand and kisses it.

"Jack, look at me." She grabs his chin and makes him face her.

"I'm not saying no. I'm just saying...not right now. Ok?"

Jack looks at her and nods, 'Ok'.

"Now, let's drink some wine. Tonight, can still be a good night, right?" She unbuttons her shirt as she kisses his neck.

She runs her hand up his thigh.

"It can most definitely still be a good night." A disappointed Jack tries not to show the depth of his hurt.

"I'll go get the wine." Jack hops up and moves over to the counter where he left a bottle of white wine chilling in a bucket of ice. As he grabs it, he notices his cellphone still recording on the counter. He quickly turns it off and shoves it in his pocket.

Virginia feels a rush of excitement as she climbs down the steps of the bus and walks toward the corner store. Today was her last day at work. She took Rita's advice and quit her job.

Virginia is carrying a shoebox filled with homemade cards from all the kids at the school.

The principal surprised her today with an assembly in her honor. Her heart smiles as she thinks of all the singing and dancing that the children did for her today.

"Hey, Ms. V!" Dante shouts as she walks into the store.

"Hey, back at ya!" Virginia shouts as she grins ear to ear.

Virginia still has told no one that she won the lottery. Especially not Dante. She wants to surprise him. Now that she has everything set up with her lawyers and the bank, she can finally share her news.

"I got a surprise for you." Virginia winks as she tosses her pork rinds onto the counter.

"What is it, Mrs. V?" Dante asks as he rings her up.

"I'm not bout to tell you right now. I'm getting the family together on Sunday, why don't you swing by?" she asks with a mischievous grin.

"What's up, D?" Dante's tall, scrawny co-worker shouts as he pushes thru double doors of the front entrance. Shane is a white boy that grew up in the neighborhood.

"How you doin, Mrs. V?" Shane trots over to Virginia and gives her a side hug.

"Hey, baby, how ya family doin?" Virginia gives Shane a quick peck on the cheek.

"They good, Mrs. V." Shane smiles as he darts behind the counter and gives Dante an up nod as he trots to the register next to Dante and clocks in.

"You late bruh," Dante says to Shane as he gives Virginia her change.

"I gotta go pick up my lil girl, bruh."

"It's three minutes, bruh. Don't be like that. You know I was wit my girl," Shane says as he winks. He and Dante chuckle and slap hands.

"Come on, Mrs. V. I'll walk you out." Dante throws up two fingers at Shane and bounces toward the door with Virginia.

He puts his arm around her and leads her out of the store. Virginia tries to keep up with him, but he causes her to step a little too quickly and twist her knee.

"You pullin' me too fast, lil boy!" Virginia stops to rub her knee.

"You know I don't move fast as I used to." Virginia gives him a pained smile as she massages her knee.

"My bad, Mrs. V. How bout I drop you off at home?" Dante points to his car.

"Boy, I'm fine. My house is only a ten-minute walk down the street. I can make it. I'll see you later, baby." Virginia waves as she starts to walk off.

She takes about two steps before feeling a sharp pain in her knee that causes her to stop in her tracks.

"Get in this car, Mrs. V." Dante chuckles as he slowly walks her to the passenger side of his car and helps her get in.

Dante hops in the driver's side and turns on the engine. Loud rap music blasts out of the speakers. Dante quickly turns the volume down.

"My bad, Mrs. V, you know I normally listen to gospel." He and Virginia laugh.

"Boy, you can tell that lie to somebody that don't know you." Virginia laughs. Dante puts the car in gear and heads out of the parking lot toward Virginia's house.

As soon as he turns out of the lot, a police car swoops into the lane and pulls up behind him with flashing lights.

"Damn!" Dante pounds his hand on the steering wheel and pulls the car over.

"It's ok, baby. You ain't did nothin. Stay calm." Virginia pats him on the shoulder.

A short, stubby white officer approaches the driver side window.

"License and registration, please," he asks.

"For what? I haven't done anything wrong," Dante says. The officer rolls his eyes.

"Can you step out of the car, sir?" the officer places his hands firmly on his belt. "Can I ask why you pulled me over, sir?" Dante asks, trying his best to keep calm.

Dante's tone makes Virginia nervous.

"You fit the description of a robbery suspect. Can you step out of the car, sir?" The cop uses his flashlight to look around the car.

"Look, I literally just got off work. I work right there at the gas station. I ain't robbed nobody, sir." Dante's voice is stern.

"I'm not going to ask you again. Step out of the car," the cop yells.

Virginia feels a lump in her throat. She remembers being Dante's age. She remembers the rage she and her friends felt when they were harassed by the police for no reason.

"Just do what he say," Virginia whispers as she nudges Dante.

Dante groans as he unbuckles his seatbelt. He slowly opens the door and steps out of the
 car.

The officer shines the flashlight in his face.

"Let me see your license, sir," the cop asks as he looks Dante up and down. Dante pulls his wallet out and yanks out his license and hands it over.

"I told you, I ain't robbed nobody. You can easily go right down the street and check with my job. I been there all day."

The cop looks over the license.

"If you haven't done anything, then why are you being so defiant? In my experience, innocent people tend to be more cooperative with police officers." He says as he eyes Dante.

"Maybe I'd be more cooperative if my civil rights weren't being violated. I'd be more cooperative if I hadn't been pulled over for no reason," Dante says assertively, his fists clenched tightly.

"Boy, you ..." the officer begins.

"Boy? Yea, there it is right there. That's really why you pulled me over. I probably look nothing like the guy you lookin for, but I bet all us boys look alike to Ya'll, huh?" Dante grits his teeth and tries not to go off on the officer.

Virginia opens her door and gets out of the car slowly.

"I'm so sorry bout this officer. My friend is going through some personal issues. He doesn't mean to take it out on you." Virginia says as she limps toward Dante.

"Get back in the car, ma'am!" the officer shouts to Virginia.

"My friend is just scared, officer. I feel like he'd feel a little less nervous if he wasn't by himself." Virginia smiles and chuckles uneasily.

"Just let the officer do what he need to do, baby. He just doing his job." Virginia makes eye contact with Dante and gives him a reassuring nod.

"Ma'am, I asked you to get back in the car." The officer eyes Virginia sternly.

"Yes, sir. I meant no disrespect. I just thought I could help. I've known this boy for fifteen years. He's a good kid. He don't mean no harm." Virginia steps away from Dante but doesn't get back in the car.

"Sir, since you wanna be so aggressive, how bout I sit you in the back of the squad car while I search your vehicle." The officer takes a step toward Dante.

"Aw naw, you ain't searchin' nothin'," Dante says as he eyes the officer.

"Tell me what I did wrong? You ain't got no proof I robbed nobody, and you need a warrant to search my property. I ain't stupid! You pulled me over to harass me, bruh. I wasn't speeding, I ain't done nothing wrong!" Dante argues.

"Calm down, baby. Just let him search the car, then we can go," Virginia pleads. Dante shakes his head as he bites his lip.

"Fine, go head and search it. You ain't gon find shit!" Dante grunts at the officer.

"Stretch out your arms, sir. I need to check you for weapons," the officer says smugly.

"Ok, but you should know my uncle is a lawyer," Dante says.

"I just want you to know that if you search me, and search my vehicle, I will be calling my lawyer.

The officer steps toward Dante and begins patting him down. As he does, Dante's emotions get the best of him. He starts to put his hand in the pocket inside his jacket. Virginia sees him reach for his pocket. She shakes her head.

The officer gets a shocked expression as Dante reaches for his pocket. He draws his weapon.

Virginia throws herself between Dante and the officer. The clap of the gunshot echoes through the air.

Virginia closes her eyes as she wraps her arms around Dante and grips him in a bear hug.

"Please don't point that gun at him! He a good kid! He don't mean no harm!" Virginia screams as she looks back at the officer whose mouth is hanging open.

He's still pointing the weapon at them.

"Mrs. V!" Dante screams as he looks at her in horror. Virginia suddenly feels a sharp pain in her back.

Dante holds Virginia as she realizes what has happened. The officer lowers his weapon.

"I need an ambulance!" the officer yells into his radio as he calls for help. Dante holds Virginia as she slowly sinks to the concrete.

"I was just reaching for my phone, Mrs. V.; I was just getting my phone." Tears stream down Dante's face as he holds Virginia.

Virginia looks up at Dante and blinks slowly as a tear rolls out of the corner of her eye.

"It's not... it's not your fault." Virginia fights to breathe.

"You one of my kids. You was always one of my kids." She gurgles as blood fills her mouth.

Virginia Johnson lays her head back as Dante cradles her.
She looks up toward the sky and stares at the stars as she draws in her last breath.

CHAPTER THREE

Jack stares at the coffin as the pallbearers remove the flowers and move it out down the center aisle of the church.

The funeral director motions for the family to rise and follow as they carry Virginia's body outside. Jack's knees buckle as he tries to stand. He stumbles as he tries to straighten up.

Rita grabs her brother and holds him up as they head out of the church. Jack locks eyes with his sister once they get outside. His face wet with tears.

"Thank you," Jack forces the words out past his sorrow.

"I don't know how you've been so strong through all this."

Tears fill Rita's eyes. She quickly wipes them away. She pulls an expensive pair of black sunglasses out of her purse and puts them on.

"I haven't been strong. I'm just doing what Mama would do." Rita's voice shakes as she speaks. She grabs her brother and hugs him.

Rita feels a tap on her shoulder and turns to face a small-statured white man with a buzz haircut. His eyes are red as tears run down his face. He looks familiar, but neither her nor Jack can remember who he is.

"I'm so sorry for your loss." The man looks as if he may double over with grief.

"Thank you. We appreciate that. You must have been a friend of our mother?" Jack extends his hand to the man.

The man grabs Jack's hand and weeps.

Rita touches the man's shoulder.

"Did you work at the school with her?" she asks.

"I'm so sorry... I'm so sorry." The man repeats himself.

Rita feels a shock through her body as a revelation clicks in her mind. She yanks Jack's hand away from the man.

"You're the cop," she says. Her body trembling with anger.

Jack blinks as he recognizes the man's face from the news stories surrounding his mother's death.

"Why would you come here?" he asks, his nostrils flaring.

"You murder our mother and you got the balls to show up at her funeral?" Jack yells, causing everyone outside to turn and look over at the altercation.

Jack snatches the man up by his collar and throws him up against the brick wall of the church banging his head against the wall. It instantly bleeds.

"Jack, Stop!" Rita yells.

"I didn't mean to shoot her." The man sobs uncontrollably.

"But you did! You did shoot her! And you came here for what? Forgiveness?" Jack's hand closes tightly around the man's neck.

Rita tries to step between them, but Jack pushes her out of the way.

"Turn'em lose, Jack! He ain't worth it, son!" the pastor calls out as he charges over to Jack.

"Don't throw your life away on this man. Virginia wouldn't want you locked up for the rest of your life," Pastor says as he slowly tries to pry Jack's hands off the man now struggling to breathe.

Jack swats the pastor away. He slams the man's head against the brick wall again and squeezes tighter and tighter. Blood pours from the back of his head.

"You came here so we could forgive you for what you did! She was everything to us!" Jack screams in his face.

His grief takes over as he breaks down in tears. Pastor Williams pulls Jack away and hugs him. The man staggers away dizzy, disoriented, and still bleeding from his head.

"We ain't never gon' forgive you! She was everything to us! Everything!" Jack shouts as he watches the man shuffle down the street.

The crowd watches the man walk away. Suddenly he stops. He sways for a moment, then collapses onto the sidewalk.

"Call an ambulance!" the pastor shouts as he rushes over to the man.

The doctor in Rita knows what has happened. She saw how hard her brother slammed the man's head into the brick wall, twice. She also saw how much blood he lost. She knows he needs to get to the hospital as soon as possible.

However, as the daughter of the woman this man just killed in cold blood last week, she remains calm. As the only doctor in the crowd, she walks slowly over to the man. A thought causes her to shiver. If this man dies, Jack will be charged with murder.

Rita kicks off her heels and races over to the man. She pulls her cell phone out of her pocket and tells the ambulance about the man's head injury. She slaps the man awake as they wait for the ambulance.

"We need to keep him alert and talking!" Rita yells as she checks his pupils. "Stay with me!" she yells.

Rita stares at the television as she curls up in her mother's favorite chair. Virginia's funeral was a week ago. So, far, this chair is the only place Rita feels anything close to peace of mind.

The news anchor on screen begins the next story:

"A police officer is under investigation after a bodycam video has surfaced showing the events that led up to the shooting of 68-year-old recent lottery winner, Virginia Johnson. In an ironic twist, the officer responsible for the shooting attended the funeral of the slain mother of three. Unfortunately, the officer suffered a savage beating once he approached the family to offer his condolences. Officer Ryan Avery suffered a severe brain injury and is currently in critical condition," the news anchor announces.

Rita grabs the remote and turns off the television. She throws the remote against the wall and it smashes into pieces.

Rita hears someone rummaging around outside the front door. She opens the door to find Sydney swaying from side to side as she digs through her purse searching for her keys. She lets out an annoyed sigh when she sees her sister standing in the doorway.

No one has seen Sydney since the family found out about Virginia's death. She never even showed up to the funeral. Sydney squints at her sister.

"Damn, why you over here?" Sydney's speech is slurred. Her eyes look droopy and she blinks slowly as if her eyelids weigh a ton.

She wears a dingy white wife beater with no bra and dirty jeans. Her once beautiful curly hair is pulled back into a matted ponytail.

Rita's nose is assaulted with the strong smell of piss and body odor. She leaves Sydney in the doorway and walks back into the house and plops back down in her mother's chair. She crosses her legs and folds her arms.

"Aw hell, what I do now? You always mad about something," Sydney mumbles and chuckles to herself as she walks in the house, shuts the door and leans against it.

"You didn't do anything." Rita shrugs and stares at her sister with her head cocked to one side.

"That's the problem, Syd! You never do anything! Maybe you forgot, but our mother died three weeks ago! Where the hell have you been? I had to handle everything. The same way that I always handle everything!" Rita snaps.

Sydney stumbles over to the couch across from Rita and sinks down onto it.

"I'm supposed to go watch them put my mama in the ground?" Sydney wipes away a tear with the back of her hand.

"You were supposed to be there with me and Jack. You owed Mama at least that! After all the hell you put her through, the absolute least you could have done is be there when they buried her!" Rita pounds her fist on the arm of the chair.

"No, I stayed away because that's what she would have wanted. You think she wanted the family, her friends, the pastor, to see her crackhead daughter?" Sydney speaks slowly and lazily.

"I ain't wanna embarrass her, again."

A knock on the door startles them both.

Rita opens the door to see Dante standing on the porch carrying a pan wrapped in aluminum foil. His head is lowered, and he has a hard time looking her in the eye.

"What are you doing here?" she asks with one hand on her hip. Dante's feet shift uncomfortably.

"My mom made ya'll a casserole. I just wanted to bring it by and let ya'll know that...um...I'm sorry for your loss." Dante's big brown eyes hold contact with Rita for a moment then look away.

"Nigga, are you kidding me? You got the nerve to show up at my mother's house and say you're sorry for our loss? She loved you like a son and you got her killed." Rita's eyes stare daggers at Dante.

Damn it, stop it, Rita!" Sydney steps in front of her sister.

"We both know there was no reason for that cop to have pulled them over in the first place! And he damn sure had no reason to pull out a gun!" Sydney leans in Rita's face.

"You need to get yo funky ass in the tub and out of my damn face!" Rita is fuming. She shakes her head.

"I can't do this."

Rita turns and marches back in the house; heads into the kitchen.

Dante bites his lips as the tears stream down his face. He backs up leans against the metal railing on the porch.

"I saw the body cam video. It wasn't your fault," Sydney says as she scratches her scalp.

"Tell your mom thank you...for the casserole. It smells amazing," Sydney says as she takes it from him.

"I ain't mean for that to happen, man. I ain't know he was gon...I ain't know." Dante tries his best to fight his tears. He wipes his face with his shirt.

"Dante, this is the same shit we see in the news every other day. This time it just happened to be somebody we love. It wasn't your fault, bruh." Sydney gives him a soft pat on his shoulder.

"Look, thanks for bringin this by." She holds up the casserole.

"Aight, you're welcome." He gives a sympathetic smile and nod as Sydney waves and shuts the door.

Rita stands at the kitchen counter sipping a glass of water as Sydney walks in the kitchen and sets the casserole pan on the counter.

"So, you're just ok with him? You don't think he had anything to do with what happened to ma?" Rita asks, placing the glass on the counter.

"I'm not ok with any of this. But I know it's not his fault ma got killed. That cop did the same thing police all across the world have been doing when they come across a black man that stands up to them. A black man that knows his rights." Sydney seats herself at the kitchen table and props her head up with her hand.

"Ok, so what about Jack? You cool with what's about to happen to Jack? You know if that officer dies, your brother is going to jail for the rest of his life, right? So, now, because Dante couldn't just shut the hell up, we lost our mother and we're probably gonna lose Jack too." Rita takes another sip of her water.

"What are you talking about?" Sydney asks shocked.

"Oh, I guess you've been too high to watch the news." Rita laughs.

"That cop brought his ass to the funeral and Jack damn near killed him. He's in the hospital in critical condition!" Rita yells.

Sydney feels her heart beating faster. "That was Jack?" she asks, wide-eyed.

"I saw something on the news about the officer in the hospital. I didn't know Jack did it." Sydney breathes deeply.

"They arrested him that night, but that lawyer girl he's with now bailed him out," Rita says unenthusiastically.

"You miss a lot when you smoke your life away, don't you?" Rita smirks.

Sheila stands in her bedroom doorway and watches as Jack sits in bed and stares at the wall deep in thought. She knocks on the door as she walks in and sits down on the edge of the bed.

"So, you ready to talk about it?" She reaches over and pats his leg.

"It really ain't nothing to talk about," Jack mumbles.

"No, there's plenty to talk about, Jack." Sheila tries to speak calmly.

"My mother was murdered. She got shot in cold blood and that officer didn't get arrested. They cleared him of all wrongdoing. You heard them on the news! He killed her and they ain't gon do nothing to him! Can we talk about that?" Jack sits up straight.

"Baby, what we need to focus on is what we're going to do if he dies. Jack, you could get charged with murder. We need to come up with a plan," Sheila urges.

"I want his ass to die! I should have murdered that son of a bitch as soon as I laid eyes on him!" Jack stares at Sheila with so much rage in his eyes that it startles her. She looks away to collect herself.

"I know you're angry and I want his ass to pay for what he did as much as you do. But I don't want you to go down for this! Your mom wouldn't want you to throw your life away. I'm asking you to see past your anger right now, baby. We need to come up with a strategy." Sheila touches his leg.

"I don't need a strategy. I need five minutes alone with that asshole to finish what I started," Jack says calmly.

Sheila fights back her tears. She slides over next to him, grabs his face and presses her forehead to his.

"Baby, I know how much you loved your mom. But I'll be damned if that man gets to take your mother's life and yours. He doesn't get to win. Baby, if you spend the rest of your life in jail, he wins," Sheila whispers to him as she wipes away his tears.

"Now, I need you to take some time to get yourself together. Don't worry about your case, baby, I got you," Sheila kisses his cheek and walks out of the room.

Rita lies in bed and pretends to be asleep as Keith slips into bed. She can smell alcohol on his breath as he slides in next to her and exhales on her neck. He runs his hands up and down her body, squeezing her breasts and kissing her neck.

"Keith, stop. I'm tired," Rita says as she elbows him off of her.

Keith is persistent. He forcefully rolls her over onto her back and continues kissing her all over as he pins her arms above her head. His eyes are red. Rita knows he's high. She heard him sniffing in the bathroom before he got into bed.

"Stop it! Get off me!" Rita kicks him and seems to wound him slightly.

This only spurs him on. Keith slaps her across the face. Rita is awestruck. He's never hit her before. He becomes aggressive with her often but has never actually hit her. She violently swings at him and lands a punch to his face. He tackles her and rips off her panties as she tries to fight him, but he's too strong. She bites his shoulder and draws blood as he holds her down, trying to penetrate her.

Keith screams out in pain. Furious, he punches her in the face.

Rita surrenders. She lays still as he enters her and pumps away. She sobs silently until he finishes. Once he's done, Keith rolls off of her and falls asleep.

A few weeks later, Rita is driving to work when her phone rings. She doesn't recognize the number but answers it anyway.

"Hello?" Rita answers.

"Hi, is this Rita Powers?" the voice on the other end asks.

"It is. How can I help you?" Rita responds.

"I'm Victoria Adams. I was your mother, Virginia Johnson's attorney. I'm so glad I finally got you. I've been trying to get in touch with you and your siblings for two weeks now." the voice says.

"Uh, I think you're mistaken. My mother never mentioned having an attorney," Rita says with a confused expression.

"Well, unfortunately, she may not have had a chance to mention it. She passed away shortly after hiring me," Victoria explains.

"Why would she hire a lawyer?" Rita questions.

"Virginia came to me looking for help setting up a trust account. She wanted to make sure that if anything happened to her, her family was taken care of. She was extremely particular and wanted everything done a certain way. I'm sure you're aware that she had recently come into a large sum of money," Victoria clarifies.

Rita is taken aback. She had barely thought of her mother's lottery win since she was killed. With everything going on with Sydney, Jack, Keith and the police officer, her life has been so chaotic she hadn't had time to think of anything else.

"Right, her money. Um yes, I remember she told me she was making plans for it. She never told me she finalized everything." Rita stumbles over her words.

"Well, she most certainly did finalize everything. She set up a trust account for you, your sister Sydney and your brother Jack. You're all listed on the account. Her name was on it as well, although she told me she didn't want her name on it. She only put her name on the account after I strongly recommended that she give herself access to her own money, for emergencies, you know." Victoria says.

"Well, wow. I didn't know. I honestly haven't had time to think about any of this. So, she left an account for each of us?" Rita asks.

"Um, no. She didn't set up an account for each of you. She set up one account for all of you. She gave explicit instructions that each of you must sign off on any withdrawals taken out of the account. There must be three signatures for every withdrawal. She was the only one who could take money out with only her signature. She also expressed that each withdrawal cannot be more than $10,000.00. There must also be at least a week between each withdrawal," Victoria elaborates.

"What? There should be about $21 million dollars in that account, right? We can only take $10,000.00 a week?" Rita fumes.

"Look, my sister and brother are always begging for money! That means I'm gonna have to meet up with them to get money out of the account every time they need something!" Rita yells in the phone.

"I'm sorry, Mrs. Powers, but I believe that's the point. Virginia told me how she wanted you guys to find a way to get along. She figured that if money was involved, maybe you'd finally come together. But she didn't want you guys to be able to just take the money out and go your separate ways. This way, even if you decide to just keep making withdrawals and drain the account, you still have to get together at least once a week." Victoria chuckles.

"Believe me, I asked her to rethink this. I told her that this might force a bigger wedge between you all."

Rita tries to think of a way to get out of the situation.

"So, you're telling me that even if I said that I don't want the money and decided to just let Sydney and Jack have it, they couldn't get to it without my signature?" Rita asks.

Victoria sighs.

"Well, your mother did have a contingency plan, just in case any of you felt that way. So, she stipulated that no money can be withdrawn without all three signatures. However, if one or all of you refuse to participate, the money will all be donated to charity. Oh, and by the way, you mentioned earlier that it was $21 million. It's actually $18.5 million. She allocated $5 million to be paid to a Dante Steward. There's also three hundred thousand set aside in a separate account for her bills that she requested be automatically paid from the account each month. Then there's two hundred thousand allocated to her church and a charity," Victoria explains.

"Hell no! Dante is not getting a dime of my mother's money! He doesn't deserve any of her money!" Rita screams into the phone.

"I'm sorry, Rita. This has already been established by Virginia. She wrote out a heartwarming letter to him that will be delivered when the check is sent out in a few weeks. She told me she thought of him as one of her children," Victoria says.

"But she..." Rita starts.

"I'm sorry to cut you off, but I'm being pulled into a meeting. We're working on a really big case. But don't worry, I'll get all the paperwork sent out to each of you. I'm so sorry about your mother. I only knew her a short time, but I can certainly see why losing her would be an extremely hard loss for you and your family. I gotta go, we'll talk soon." Victoria hangs up the phone.

Rita takes the phone away from her ear and stares at it in disbelief.

A few days later, Rita stares at herself in her bathroom mirror as she inhales deeply. She closes the lid of the toilet and takes a seat on the toilet. She notices her hands are shaking, she squeezes them together to stop the shaking. She inhales again to calm herself. She reaches over to the sink and picks up the pregnancy test sitting there. She bites her lip before she checks the results.

She feels a chill roll through her body as she sees the word "pregnant" on the small screen.

She knew it, though she didn't want to believe it was true. Her period was due to start last week, but when it never did, she had blamed it on stress until her nipples began feeling sore.

Rita hears the front door of her condo open and shut. Keith is home. She hyperventilates as she leans over the bathroom sink. She taps her foot, trying to regain control of her body. She splashes water on her face and focuses on her eyes in the mirror.

Ever since the night he forced himself on her, she can't bring herself to look at him. Yes, he was drunk and high, but she's been using that as an excuse to justify his behavior for years.

She throws the test in the trash and pulls the trash bag out of the can and ties it tightly. She throws open the bathroom door to find Keith sitting on the bed. He unbuttons his shirt and kicks off his shoes and puts his feet up on the bed. Rita can tell by his eyes, he's not high yet.

"Hey," he says, as he grabs the remote and turns on the television.

"Hey," Rita responds in a dry tone as she walks out of the room with the bag and into the kitchen; where she puts it in the larger trash can. She pulls the bag out of the kitchen trash can, ties it and puts it outside the front door for the maintenance man to pick up.

She walks back into the bedroom and stares at her husband. He doesn't notice she's there. He's focusing intently on his cellphone.

She thinks back to when they met in college. She remembers how caring he used to be. He always had an arrogance to him, but she found it charming. He started using soon after they finished med school. He met these two white boys he studied with. They would invite him to parties where they passed the stuff around like candy. Keith wanted so badly to fit in with the other doctors. Many of the young docs were using and didn't seem to have any problems. At first, it was just recreational. He only used occasionally with his doctor friends at parties. Then it became every weekend, then slowly over the years, it became daily a habit. She longed for the sweet, handsome, intelligent man she met all those years ago.

"I think we need to talk." Rita's voice makes Keith glance up sharply from his phone. "What is it?" he asks.

"I feel that we should separate for a while. I'm not happy. I don't think you are either," Rita starts.

"Wait... you don't have to do this," Keith says.

"I've made up my mind. I'm moving out. I've just been waiting for the right time to tell you. Honestly, I was waiting for a moment when you were sober," Rita continues.

"Look, I got it under control. I don't even use as much as I used to. I'm cutting back. I promise. We can get through this. I know it's been a rough couple years but, I still love you, Ri," Keith says sincerely.

He gets up and walks over to Rita.

"See, that doesn't work for me. I don't need you to cut back, Keith. I need it to stop. I never know who I'm coming home to at night. I'm just waiting for the call that someone has found you dead because you've overdosed. I hate to even think this, but at least then I would be able to stop worrying! Keith, I can't be in a marriage where I'm praying that my husband ODs!" Rita says sharply.

"I'm gonna get it together. I promise, baby. I promise you." Keith wraps his arms around his wife and hugs her tightly.

Rita stands there limp as he squeezes her. She can't bring herself to hug him back.

"I want you to get it together. I promise I do. I just can't stay here while you do it." Rita breaks free of the hug and goes into the closet and packs her suitcase.

Sydney rocks back and forth on the sofa she used to share with her mother. They would sit up at night, sipping sweet tea and watching Virginia's nightly line up on TV. Now Sydney sits alone in the old house. Every inch of it reminds her of her mother. She's been trying her best to stay clean like she promised Virginia she would. Sydney ran out of drugs yesterday and decided to get clean cold turkey. But that's mostly because she's broke. Her skin is moist with sweat and she can't seem to stop shaking.

Sydney picks up her cellphone as she paces the floor. Her mother's lawyer called her the day before and explained the trust account. She knows there's only one way to get the money.

She scrolls through her contacts and finds Rita's name and presses "Call."

"What do you need, Syd?" Rita asks flatly.

"Why do you always think I need something? I'm just calling to see how you doin," Sydney lies.

"Because you always need something, Sydney. You never call me unless you need something. How much do you need?" Rita rolls her eyes as she waits for the response.

Sydney paces the floor.

"Damn, I just. It's not like that this time," she tries to explain. "So, you don't need money," Rita asks.

"Look, I just need you to come down to the bank with me tomorrow. I need money for an apartment or something. I just can't stay in this house anymore," Sydney says, half lying.

It's true that she wants to get out of the house, but she and Rita both know what she will do as soon as she gets the money.

"How are you planning to rent an apartment without a job?" Rita presses, trying to poke a hole in the lie.

Sydney hadn't thought of that. She pauses, silently searching for a response.

"Um, I don't know. Maybe you can help me. Jack told me you offered him a job. Maybe I could work for you." Sydney is proud of how fast she thought of that. She knows Rita would die before she let her drugged-out sister come work at her fancy midtown office.

"You know what, ok. I'll get you a job at my office. I'll even help you get an apartment," Rita replies.

Sydney stops pacing.

"Wait, so you're gonna let me come work for you? Seriously?" Sydney asks.

"Yep, if you check yourself into a rehab program. Not just going to meetings, Syd. I want you checked into a good program for at least 30 days. Once you show me you can do that, then yea, I'll help you," Rita says sternly.

"See, I knew it! Why do you always do this to me, Rita? I don't need rehab! I can take care of myself!" Sydney screams.

She plops down on the sofa.

"Look, I'll figure out the apartment thing on my own. I just need you to come to the bank with me and Jack tomorrow so I can get some money out of Mama's trust account to help me get started. Can you just do that?" Sydney asks as humbly as she can.

"Fine. I'll do it," Rita concedes.

"Just don't kill yourself with that shit." Rita hangs up the phone.

The next day, Rita pulls into the parking lot in front of her office. She told her assistant she'd be late. She'd met up with Sydney and Jack as she promised. She told them they could split the ten thousand. Little was said at the meeting. Jack seemed solemn and depressed. Sydney looked pale and sickly, but at least she was clean.

Rita's assistant, Trish, spots her car pull up and runs outside. She has a panicked look on her face. Rita gets out of her car.

"Girl, you ok?" Rita asked jokingly.

"Dr. Powers, there's something going on with your husband. He's making the patients very uncomfortable. I know he's a doctor and I didn't want to question him, but something is not right," Trish says frantically.

"What do you mean?" Rita's heart is racing. She knew this would happen eventually.

"He's slurring his words. His eyes are red. When I came in this morning, he was passed out on the couch in his office. Dr. Powers, he smells like alcohol and he's making the patients uncomfortable. If I'm being honest, he makes me uncomfortable," Trish explains nervously.

"I'll take care of it. It all sounds like side effects of his new medication. I told you he has a health condition. I told him to take some time off while he adjusts to the meds, but you know how these men are, girl. Don't worry, I'll deal with it," Rita lies.

She can feel the rage bubbling up inside her as she walks into the office. Her eyes search quickly for Keith. She spots him walking into his office. She quickly follows him inside and closes the door behind them.

"Ah, my wife finally shows up," Keith says as he sits in his desk chair. "You need to get the fuck out of here!" Rita whispers forcefully.

"Look at you! You're wrinkled and you stink! Your eyes are bloodshot red. There is alcohol seeping out of your pores, I can smell you from here." Rita looks him up and down in horror.

"I look fine. I might be a little wrinkled, but I'm fine," Keith says, trying his best not to slur his words.

"Then why did Trish just stop me in the parking lot to tell me that my husband, a doctor, is walking around practicing medicine smelling like a frat boy?" Rita scolds him in a low tone so no one outside the door can hear her.

"You are destroying everything we worked for years trying to build! Now, I made an excuse for you. You are leaving, right now!" She points to the door.

"Fine. I don't have to stay here and deal with this shit! And you can tell that nosey ass assistant of yours to mind her damn business!" Keith shouts. He stands up and storms out of the office.

Rita is mortified. She knows everyone heard him, patients, staff, everyone. Trish tiptoes into Keith's office and closes the door behind her. Rita sinks into Keith's desk chair and hides her face in her hands. She breathes deeply, trying to stop the tears from flowing.

Trish pats Rita on the back.

"It's ok, girl. We've all been there with men. It doesn't matter if he's a doctor or a mechanic. If he's an asshole, he's an asshole," Trish chuckles.

Rita looks up at Trish and smiles, she's grateful for the support.

"There is something I need to speak with you about though, Dr. Powers. Please don't be upset with me.

Yesterday, we received a big order of samples for that new pain medication. I stocked them all in the drug cabinet and locked it. I swear I locked it! But this morning when I came in, the cabinet door was opened a little and they were all gone." Trish sinks down onto the couch next to Keith's desk. Rita exhales sharply and lowers her head onto the desk.

"That son of a bitch," she mumbles under her breath.

Dante approaches Mrs. Virginia's house. The front door is slightly opened. He looks around suspiciously before nudging it open and peering inside. Sydney is passed out on the couch. She's wearing red panties and a black tank top. One of her small breasts peers out of the side of the disheveled tank top as she sleeps.

"Syd...Syd?" Dante calls over to her from the doorway.

Sydney rolls over onto her stomach but doesn't wake. Her bare bottom on display through her thong panties. Dante moves closer to her and grabs a blanket from the chair near the couch. He tosses it over her to cover her up. He moves back to the doorway and knocks loudly.

The sound jolts Sydney out of her sleep.

"Sorry, I ain't mean to scare you. The door was cracked open," Dante says, his eyes shifting from Sydney to the floor and back.

Sydney sits up and wraps herself in the blanket.

"It's cool. What's up?" she asks groggily.

Dante shifts uneasily from one foot to the other.

"I got this in the mail" he says. His hands shaking as he holds out a large tan envelope. Sydney notices the pain in his face.

"That from Mama's lawyer?" Sydney knows what it is without looking at it.

Dante lets his arm fall to his side, the envelope still clutched in his hand. He shakes his head, yes.

"She told me...that night...she told me she had something to tell me. She invited me over to dinner." Dante's voice quivers.

Sydney can see how broken he is. He looks like he hasn't slept in days. His once light- hearted spirit now seems so heavy.

She leans into him.

"She wanted you to have that money. She loved you, 'Te. Do you know how much she talked about you?" Sydney reaches over and pats his leg.

"I killed her! Mrs. V treated me like her son, and I got her killed!" Dante grunts. "I can't take this money, Syd." Dante drops his head into his hands and sobs.

"Yes, you can. You have to stop blaming yourself for her death. It wasn't your fault. We don't blame you for what happened." Sydney moves over to him and holds his hand as he cries.

"Rita does. She told me it was my fault." Dante forces the words out through labored breaths.

"Every time I blink, I see yo mama face." He moans as he tries to hold back sorrowful tears.

"I can't take her money." Dante stands up and rips the envelope in half. The pieces scatter to the floor around his feet.

Sydney walks over and picks them up. She digs through the ripped envelope and finds the check is still intact. She pulls it out and holds it up to him.

"Fuck Rita," Sydney says sternly.

"She don't speak for the whole family. Mama wanted you to have this money. She loved you and she believed in you. You have a daughter to take care of. Do you know how much this money could change your life? You are keeping this check." Sydney grabs his hand and places the check inside.

Dante lowers his head as the tears continue to flow. Sydney touches his chin and lifts his face.

"Stop it. It was not your fault." Sydney leans in and kisses his cheek. She wipes the tears from his face and kisses his lips.

Dante places the check on the coffee table, turns and walks out.

Sheila leads Sydney to her master bedroom door.

"He's in there." Sheila gestures toward her bedroom door. Sydney gives her a grateful nod and pushes the door open. Jack is sitting in bed staring at the television.

"Hey big brother." Sydney walks in and flops down on the bed and flashes smile.

"I've been worried about you. You haven't been answering your phone," Sydney says.

"Sorry, Syd. I just ain't felt like talking to nobody. Needed some time to myself," Jack responds halfheartedly.

"Yea, I know. Sheila told me. She said she can't get you to leave the house." Sydney eyes her big brother.

"I messed up, Syd. I messed up and I let Mama down." The words come out as if it hurts him to speak.

"You couldn't have let Mama down. You were her favorite. You know that right?" Sydney jokes.

"I shouldn't have grabbed him. I just didn't expect to see him at the funeral, then all of a sudden, he's standing in my face. The man that killed my mama showed up to her funeral." Jack forces the words out.

"He deserved to get his ass beat!" Sydney says sharply.

"He had no business coming to the funeral of the woman he murdered. Whether he meant to do it or not! You didn't let Mama down, you stood up for our mother! She would be proud that her son stood up for her." Sydney stands up and puts one hand on her thin hip.

Jack looks up at his sister. The pain in his face eases but does not go away.

"Ok. But who side you think that judge gon be on? I'm goin to jail, Syd. I'm goin to jail for the rest of my life for killing that man. You heard the news, he ain't gon wake up out that coma." Jack nods his head like it's a fact.

"No, you're not!" Sheila bursts through the door.

"I just got a call from my friend at the hospital. He just woke up." Sheila places her hand over her racing heart.

Sydney flies across the bed and hugs her brother. "I knew it!" Sydney laughs as she squeezes him.

Jack's eyes widen in disbelief. He's frozen. He lets Sydney hug him, but he doesn't move. He thought for sure his life was over. As the emotion washes over him, he smiles. He smiles a genuine grin for the first time since his mother died. He lifts his arms and hugs Sydney.

Sheila crosses over to him. Sydney notices her there, gives her brother a quick peck on the cheek and hops up to make way for Sheila.

Sheila sits next to him, strokes his face and kisses him. He grabs her hands and kisses each one.

"We still have our work cut out for us. But at least we know it won't be a murder charge. They'll try to throw assault and battery at you, but that's a cake walk. We got this, boo." Sheila wraps her arms around him and lets out a relieved sigh.

Rita rushes around the office. It's only noon and she's already exhausted. She still hasn't told Keith about the child she's carrying. By her calculations, she's about eight weeks along. The nausea has set in. She tries her best to hide the vomiting and fatigue. It's been easier to hide it from Keith since she's been living out of a hotel for the last three weeks.

"You have a pretty light afternoon, Dr. Powers. You only had two appointments after lunch and one just rescheduled. You should be done by two o'clock," Trish, Rita's assistant, says.

"Thank God," Rita says as she sinks down onto the couch in her office. She kicks off her heels and puts her feet up on the couch.

"Girl, are you ok?" Trish gives Rita a sideways glance.

"I'm good. I'm just tired. I might cancel tomorrow. When was the last time I took a few days off?" Rita lays her head back on the arm of the couch and closes her eyes.

"Since when do you take a few days off?" Trish asks.

Rita chuckles.

"Well, damn, I guess that means I'm overdue for a break, huh?"

Trish inches her way closer to the sofa. She tosses her long dark hair weave over her shoulder and pats the top of her head with her hand. She puts the other hand on her hip.

"Uh, huh. Are you sure there's no other reason why you're so tired?" Trish asks, pursing her lips together.

Rita opens her eyes and looks suspiciously at her assistant. "Are you implying something, Patricia?" she asks slyly.

"All I'm saying is, you're just looking very tired and sluggish lately. And, If I'm not mistaken, your lunch has made you nauseous at least twice this week." Trish raises her eyebrows.

"Keith is right, you are nosey as hell." Rita rolls her eyes and smiles.

"I'm not trying to be nosey. All I'm saying is, I'm very happy for you." Trish slides in and gives Rita a quick pat on her tummy.

"Girl, get out of my office!" Rita laughs. Trish winks at her and turns to leave.

"Trish, can you keep this to yourself. My husband doesn't know yet. I'm um, trying to surprise him." Rita pleads with her eyes.

"Oh, that's so sweet. Of course, I won't say anything," Trish says as she walks out.

Rita pulls up in front of her mother's house. Just the sight of the old house brings her comfort. She can't even verbalize how much she misses being able to drive to her mother's house and have dinner. She smiles as she pictures Mrs. Virginia fussing as she walks around the kitchen complaining about how everyone was too lazy to get up and help her cook.

Then, as soon as someone tried to help, she would scream about how they were doing it wrong. Rita parks her car in the driveway and leans her head back against the headrest. She inhales deeply as she remembers her childhood. She remembers playing on the front porch as a kid, then sitting with her mother as Virginia rocked back and forth in her rocking chair.

A raggedy looking man walks out of the front door. He's adjusting his dingy clothes as he heads down the front steps and bounces away from the house. Rita has never seen him before. She quickly opens her door and hops out of the car. Rita rushes up the front steps and pushes the front door open.

As she opens the door, she sees that a man is on top of a naked, passed out Sydney. He's holding her legs up as he pumps away on top of her. Sydney looks half-dead as the man has his way with her. Her eyes are closed and her body limp, but the man doesn't seem to notice or mind.

Rita sees red.

"Get the fuck off of her!" she screams at the top of her lungs. She snatches open the closet near the front door where her dad always kept an old metal baseball bat. Rita grabs the bat and holds it out straight, pointing it at the man.

"Ok, ok! Hold up, Rita! Put the bat down!" The man jumps up and grabs his clothes laying at his feet.

Rita looks confused. Then recognizes him as one of the guys she grew up with in the neighborhood.

Rita doesn't back down.

"I walk in and find you raping my sister and you tell me to put the bat down! Nigga, I will kill you!" Rita yells.

"No, no, no! I wasn't raping her! She was having fun. She wanted to do it! She just fell asleep before we finished." The guy pleaded his case as he shimmies into his jeans.

Rita pounds the bat against the wall.

"Get the fuck out of my mama's house, Craig!" Rita says, finally remembering his name.

Craig grabs a small bag of white powder from the coffee table and runs out of the front door. Rita closes the door behind him and locks it. The slam of the door causes Sydney to drowsily open her eyes. She looks up at Rita and tries to figure out what's happening.

Rita is furious.

"So, you just let these dope heads come and go as they please in Mama's house?"

Sydney mumbles incoherently. Her eyes roll back and forth in her head. She blinks slowly at her sister.

"I cannot believe this shit. You can't just have crack heads running in and out this house!" Rita tosses a blanket at Sydney who's too out of it to cover herself.

Sydney fights to sit up but can only manage to prop herself up on the arm of the couch. She rests her head there and licks her dry, ashy lips as she tries to speak.

"I can't have my friends over?" she says. Her voice is hoarse and crackling.

Tired of looking at her sister's boney, naked body, Rita walks over to her and covers her with the blanket.

"You are fucking pathetic." Rita laughs to herself.

"You don't even have enough respect for your parents not to do this in their house? Look, I don't care if you wanna hoe yourself out, but I'll be damned if you turn this house into a crack house!" Rita says as she kicks trash away from her feet.

The floor is littered with old syringes, dirty clothes and old food wrappers.

"So, I'm pathetic?" Sydney croaks. She lifts herself into a seated position.

"What about you? My boy told me he sold your husband some rock bout a week ago." Sydney wipes the crust out of her eyes.

Rita feels her heart stop for what feels like an eternity. She had dreaded the day her husband and Sydney would cross paths in the streets, but she knew it would happen one day. Keith was getting more and more careless as the addiction took hold of him.

"You ain't got nothin to say now, huh?" Sydney mocks.

Rita composes herself.

"I don't know who your friend saw, but it wasn't Keith. He's a doctor, Sydney. Don't let your friends lie about my husband," Rita says sharply.

"You think I don't know a dope fiend when I see one? You said yourself I'm a crack head, right? Every time I see that nigga he looks high." Sydney smiles.

Rita suddenly feels nauseous. She hops out of the recliner and runs to the bathroom. She stands over the toilet and pauses as she feels her lunch rise up in her throat. She tries to breathe and keep the inevitable from happening. The toilet is disgusting and looks like Sydney hasn't cleaned it in a month or more. The sight of it causes her to give in to the feeling and hurl.

Once she's done, she leans over the sink and steadies herself. Rita turns on the faucet and uses her hand to scoop water into her mouth. She swishes it around her mouth and spits it out. She looks up at herself in the mirror and sees Sydney standing behind her.

"You ok?" Sydney pulls on a black tank top and rests herself against the doorway.

"I'm good. I just got a little light-headed. I've been working too hard, I think," Rita lies as she straightens her clothes, grabs a small towel on the counter, and wipes her face.

"I knew you were starting to look a little chunky." Sydney smirks and shakes her head. "When are you due?" she asks smugly. "Who said I was pregnant?" Rita is determined to keep the lie going.

Sydney rolls her eyes.

"And you say I'm pathetic. You knew you were married to a drug addict and you let him get you pregnant? But I'm pathetic? I bet you never called him pathetic though, huh?" Sydney scoffs.

Rita pushes past Sydney and stomps out of the bathroom. She remembers how Keith had pinned her down and raped her the night their child was conceived. Sydney follows Rita into the living room.

Rita paces the floor furiously.

"Keith is not some crack head! He is a respected physician! So, what if he pops some pills every now and then. You will never understand how stressful it is to be a doctor, you broke ass bitch! Your ass has never even had a real job!"

Sydney tries to speak, but Rita's not done yet.

"You used to be so smart! You made straight A's all through school! Now look at you, you can't even take care of yourself! You are a child! You got niggas coming in and out this house running trains on you! You can't even wash your ass!" Rita rants.

Sydney seats herself on the couch while Rita stomps around. She picks up a half-empty beer bottle from the coffee table and takes a swig. Rita tires herself out and plops down in her mother's recliner.

Sydney chuckles.

"I'm glad you finally said it. You been holding all that in for years, huh? I guess now that Mama's gone, you ain't gotta play nice no more." Sydney sips her beer.

Rita feels the slight sting of guilt. Although she meant everything she said, she knew most of that anger was about Keith, not Sydney.

"Look, I didn't mean to..." Rita starts, but Sydney quickly cuts her off.

"Naw, don't worry about it. I'm glad you got it off your chest." Sydney grins sarcastically and stands up.

"Now let me go wash my ass." Sydney shoots Rita an evil glare as she walks out of the room.

CHAPTER FOUR

Jack rushes around the kitchen as he quickly fixes a plate for Sheila. It's taken a few weeks, but he has finally been able to somewhat pull himself out of that dark place he was in.

Sheila was a big part of that. If not for her, Jack knows he'd probably still be in jail. She's been doing everything she can to work on his case while also fighting to keep him sane.

Jack has spent the last few hours cooking. He made homemade lasagna, a salad and rolls. The lasagna was his mother's recipe.

"Baby, that smells amazing!" Sheila says, walking into the kitchen.

Jack takes her hand and leads her to the dining room table. He pulls out her chair and helps her sit.

"Let's just hope it tastes as good as it smells." Jack flashes a smile that Sheila hasn't seen in a long time. He leans in and softly kisses her cheek.

Sheila blushes as she watches Jack turn and walk over to the kitchen counter. It's been a long time since a man cared for her the way this man does. He's gentle with her. He's attentive and affectionate. Sheila thinks back to the night he proposed to her. She's regretted turning him down every day since.

She never wanted to hurt him, but she had to protect herself. For some reason she always ends up with these men who can't take care of themselves and try to use her for her money. When Jack proposed, she knew that she loved him, but she was afraid that they would get married and she would take care of him throughout their entire marriage.

So, she said no. She had to make sure she wasn't just saying yes to good sex and some company. Sheila has been letting men walk all over her all her life. Before she met Jack, she told herself that pattern was over. Next thing she knew, he lost his job and was moving in with her until he got on his feet.

Sheila knows he's a good man, but she needs him to show her he has some ambition. Show her he can take care of himself and her if she ever needed him to. She prays that she didn't scare him out of ever wanting to propose to her again.

Jack sits a plate of food down in front of her. He drapes a cloth napkin across her lap. Jack takes a seat across from her.

"Here's to good women." He holds up his glass and clinks it against hers.

Sheila blushes.

"And good men." She smiles.

A loud knock startles them. Jack hops up and goes to the front door.

"You Jack Johnson?" a loud aggressive voice asks.

Sheila jumps up from the table. She was afraid this would happen.

"Uh, yea. Can I help you?" Jack asks with uncertainty.

"Sir, you're under arrest! Put your hands behind your back!" The officer shouts as he slams Jack against the wall.

Two other officers follow him in with guns drawn as they look around the living room.

"You do not have a warrant to search my home!" Sheila shouts as one officer tries to push past her and go down the hall toward the bedrooms.

The officer tries to push past her again, but she jumps in his way.

"Sir, I am a lawyer! I know my rights! When I'm done pressing charges, I'll have your damn badge mounted on my mantel!"

Sheila steps back and puts both hands squarely on her hips.

The officer backs off.

"Now what's the damn charge?" Sheila asks firmly.

"Assault and battery," the officer holding Jack against the wall says gruffly.

"I knew that was coming. Don't worry, baby. I'll have you out by the morning," Sheila says confidently.

Jack nods and tries to keep his head up as the officers walk him out.

Sheila slams the door behind them and kicks it once it closes. As the tears fill her eyes, she leans back against the door. She slides down to the floor. She expected them to come after him again now that new charges have been brought forth.

Sheila exhales deeply and gathers herself.

She pushes herself off of the floor and goes over to the couch and digs through her purse for her cell phone. She quickly dials her assistant's number.

"Hey, Corey. We're going to have to get this court case moved up. They've arrested Jack again. They're not gonna stop coming after him until something sticks. Dig up everything you can on that officer. I'll call you later."

Sheila hangs up the phone, slides on a pair of flip flops, grabs her purse and walks out the door.

Rita is draped across the couch in her office. She's kicked off her shoes and has a warm towel on her face. It's four o'clock and the last patient just left. It's been a long day. Since Keith has become more and more unreliable, she's had to treat most of his patients.

Sometimes he doesn't show up for days at a time. When he does show up, Rita does her best to make sure he treats as little patients as possible. She can't risk someone figuring out that he's high.

Trish bursts into the office. She looks shaken and confused.

"Dr. Powers, um, there are a bunch of federal agents at the front desk. They said they need to search the office!" Trish says frantically.

Rita leaps up from the sofa.

"What? Federal agents? Did they say why they need to search?" Rita asks the question but already knows the answer.

"No, they just want to talk to you and Keith!" Trish is clearly about to fall apart. Rita grabs her shoulders.

"Just breathe, girl. We've done nothing wrong. I'm sure it's just a routine thing." Rita takes a deep breath to hide her own nerves.

She walks out of the office and down the hall to the front desk. She's immediately thrown as she sees at least ten agents staring back at her with stern faces. They're all in black jackets. Some jackets have DEA printed on them; the others say FBI.

"Can I help you?" Rita asks, trying to stop her voice from shaking.

A female agent steps forward and extends her hand to shake. Rita almost mistook the small box-shaped agent for a man. She had on no makeup and her hair was pulled back under an FBI cap.

"Yes, Dr. Rita Powers? I'm Agent Thomas," the agent says firmly.

"Yes, I'm Dr. Rita Powers. Nice to meet you." Rita shakes her hand cautiously.

"Nice to meet you, Dr. Powers. Is the other Dr. Powers here also? We were hoping to speak with him as well," she asked as she looked around.

"No, he's not feeling well. He wasn't able to come in today," Rita lies.

Can I ask what this is about?" Rita demands.

"Dr. Powers, we have a warrant to search your office. We have reason to suspect fraud related to the drugs prescribed by your husband. Your husband has also requested several large quantities of pain medications from pharmaceutical representatives. We've been watching your office for a few weeks now. Based on the size of this office and the number of patients you see... something just isn't adding up." The short stubby agent takes off her cap and smooths her hair back.

"I have no idea what you're talking about. Prescription fraud? This is a reputable business! We built this practice from the ground up! Do you know hard we worked to put ourselves through medical school? I cannot believe this! Do you know we are the only African American run practice in the area? Do you understand what an allegation like this will do to our practice?" Rita screams, but she knows it's all falling on deaf ears.

She's suddenly overwhelmed with nausea. Her head is light, and her heart is racing. Feeling as if she might faint, she grips the counter. Trish grabs Rita's arm and holds her up. She helps Rita to a nearby chair and seats her there.

Another agent steps forward. The tall dark-skinned man puts his hand on Rita's shoulder.

"We do understand that," he says.

That's why we came in unmarked cars and we waited until all of your patients left." He nods reassuringly.

"This is just a standard investigation. It happens occasionally at doctors' offices. If we find nothing, this all goes away quietly," Agent Thomas says calmly.

"Ok. Well, I appreciate your discretion. Do what you have to do." Rita waves them off.

The agents split up and search every room in the office. Rita feels a lump form in her throat as she spots one of them heading into Keith's office.

"It's over," she whispers to herself as she rubs her belly.

Later that night, Rita is lying in bed at the hotel where she's been staying for the past month. She tosses and turns, unable to sleep as she thinks of her office being ransacked by federal agents.

She's tried over and over again to call Keith, but he hasn't answered her calls or responded to her texts. She hears her phone buzzing on the nightstand and hops out of bed, hoping he's finally calling her back. She rolls her eyes when she sees Sydney's name on the screen.

Rita reluctantly answers the phone. "What, Syd?"

"Well, damn, hello to you too," Sydney snaps back.

"Sydney, it's 10:30 at night. I was in bed. Why are you calling so late?" Rita rolls her eyes as if her sister can see her.

"Alright look, I need you and Jack to go to the bank with me tomorrow morning. I need to take out some more money." Sydney sighs as she awaits Rita's response.

"Seriously? I went to the bank with ya'll three weeks ago, Syd! I let you and Jack split ten thousand dollars. You spent five thousand dollars in three weeks?" Rita yells into the phone.

"I had a few things to come up, Ri! Look, I owed some people money. I'm broke and I'm hungry. I don't need you to judge me right now! I need help!" Sydney pleads sincerely.

"Oh, you owed people money?" Rita chuckles.

"You couldn't just sell your ass like you usually do?" Rita says viciously. Sydney bites her lip to keep from cursing her sister out.

"Damn, Rita. it's not even your money I'm asking for this time! Its Mama's money and she left it to all of us, not just you!" Sydney responds.

"Oh, I'm well aware that it's Mama's money! And you know what, I'm gonna say what she should have said while she was alive, hell no! I ain't giving you no damn money! Once I see that you're actually making an effort to better yourself and get clean, then we can talk about this money. But today, no. You ain't getting shit! I'm not helping you kill yourself, Syd! I am done enabling you! Good night!" Rita hangs up the phone and tosses it back onto the nightstand.

Sydney stares at her phone as the call disconnects. She looks around the dimly lit house that once made her feel loved and secure. Since her mother died, the house feels cold and empty. She walks into the kitchen and opens the refrigerator that used to be overflowing with food. Sydney eyes the empty shelves and slams the door.

She pulls open the pantry door and searches for anything she can eat. A jar of peanut butter causes her eyes to swell up with tears. She grabs the jar and fishes a spoon out the drawer near the sink.

She plops down at the kitchen table and shovels the peanut butter into her mouth.

A vision of her mother rushing around the kitchen the way she used to flashes before her eyes. She remembers Virginia standing over the stove frying chicken and then whipping homemade mashed potatoes.

The tears flow down her cheeks as she licks peanut butter from the spoon.

Rita pulls into the parking lot of her office the next day. She notices the "We're Closed" sign still in the window. She sighs loudly as she thinks of how often she's had to remind Trish to take the sign out of the window after she opened in the mornings.

Rita notices two unmarked cars sitting in the parking lot.

Agents in DEA and FBI jackets are huddled together talking and eyeing paperwork in manila folders. As Rita pulls up, they spread out and watch her with stern faces.

The short, stocky agent that Rita had mistaken for a man the day before steps forward. She meets Rita as she gets out of the car.

"Dr. Powers, I'm sure you remember me from yesterday. I'm Agent Thomas." She greets Rita.

Rita tries not to look nervous, but the severity of the situation is written all over their faces.

"Good morning, I assume you were able to complete your investigation? I'll have patients arriving in an hour. I can't have federal agents hanging around my office." Rita forces a nervous smile.

"Unfortunately, we haven't finished. While going through your records, we found several red flags. I'm sorry, Dr. Powers, but we can't allow you to open your office until we've completed our investigation." Agent Thomas hands Rita a legal document.

Rita feels her heart sink.

"What? I have a business to run. I can't just shut down like that without giving any sort of notice to my patients," Rita pleads.

"You don't have a choice. Both you and your husband's medical licenses are suspended until we sort this out," Agent Thomas says sternly as she turns and walks back to the other agents.

Rita feels as if the wind has been knocked out of her.

She fumbles with her keys as she tries to unlock her car door. Her hands are shaking so badly that she drops the keys on the ground. She quickly picks them up and breathes deeply to calm herself. Her shaking slows, allowing her to open the door.

She slams the door and reaches over to grab a McDonald's bag with a sausage biscuit and a hash brown she purchased for her breakfast this morning. She opens the bag, leans over and retches into the bag.

She tries to keep her head below the dashboard so the agents wouldn't see. Then she began to wonder if it would even matter at this point. She grabs napkins from her glove compartment and wipes her mouth.

She digs around in her purse and pulls out her cell phone. It shows a missed call from Keith.

Her heart is beating out of her chest as she calls him.

"Where the hell have you been?" She screams when he answers.

"Look, you're the one who decided to move out. You said you didn't want to be with me. I don't have to answer the phone every time you call," Keith says angrily.

"Do you know what the hell is going on at our office? The gotdamn feds have shut down the office because of prescription fraud! What the fuck have you been doing Keith!" Rita starts the car and pulls out of the parking lot.

"They did what...?" Keith can barely get it out before Rita screams in his ear again.

"Prescription fraud, nigga! Both of our licenses are suspended! I can't practice medicine until this is over! This is exactly what I told you would happen!" Rita fumes.

"Wait, wait. Slow down! I don't understand, what?" Keith fumbles over his words as he tries to sort out what his wife is telling him.

"Keith, you are going to come clean with them! I don't give a damn what you've been doing, but I can't have my license suspended. You will tell them that I had nothing to do with any of it!" Rita speeds down the highway as she talks.

"Just calm down! They probably have no proof that anything has happened. They only suspect fraud. If they had proof, I'd be in jail. Let them do the investigation. I was careful, Rita. They won't find any evidence." Keith does his best to sound sure.

Rita calms herself.

"Ok, Keith. But what if they do find something?" she asks calmly.

"What if we both lose our license and our practice is shut down permanently? Are you seriously, willing to risk me losing everything, when you know I had nothing to do any of it? Before they try to arrest both of us, I need you to be honest. Tell them the truth! Be a man and do your time. When you get out, if you're clean, maybe I'll let you be a part of your child's life." Rita swallows hard as she finally tells him about the child growing in her womb.

Keith falls silent.

"My child? You're pregnant?" Keith asks.

"Yes. I honestly didn't know if I would ever tell you about it. I told you I didn't want to have a child with you while you were on this shit. I didn't know if you were ever going to get clean. For a while I thought about having an abortion. Look, I want this baby, Keith. I'm forty-three years old, I refuse to miss out on my chance to have a baby because of your ass!" Rita cries.

"I need my license so that I can provide for this child. You need to do the right thing," Rita begs.

"Baby, I want this child too. You know I always wanted a baby. I'm gonna get us out of this. I promise. I'm gonna get clean, and I'll get us out of this. I'm gonna fix this." Keith's voice trembles as he speaks.

Rita can hear the sincerity in his voice.

"Fix it," Rita says sharply as she hangs up the phone.

Sydney quickly slides into the corner store while Dante is busy talking to a customer. She does her best not to be noticed as she moves from aisle to aisle. Sydney grabs a pack of ham slices out of the cooler and hurriedly shoves it down her pants. Next she snatches a package of cheese.

She feels her stomach growling as she glides down the aisles. She's still broke and since Rita refuses to help her get money out of the bank, she feels her only options are to steal or starve. She's tired of selling her body to disgusting men for cash or dope.

It used to be easy to turn her mind off, let them do their business, collect the cash and go about her day. The death of her mother awakened something in her. Lately, her mind is filled with thoughts of how her mother died knowing that her daughter was a drug addict and a prostitute. Her mother died before she got the chance to turn into a real person.

She stuffs candy bars and a soda into her jacket before easing her way to the door. Dante is just finishing up with his customer.

"What up, Syd?" He gives her an up nod. Sydney flashes a shy grin.

"What's up, D? Ya'll still ain't got my Ranch Pringles in here, huh? I'll go check across the street," she says as she makes her way to the door.

"Nah, we ain't got the ranch flavor. What about all that shit you stuffed in your pockets though?" he asks with a smile as he walks around the counter to stand face to face with her.

Sydney fidgets awkwardly.

"I'm sorry. Uh, I just didn't have... I was gonna pay you back." Sydney breaks down. Her tears spill out as she empties her pockets.

"You know you can ask me if you need something. I don't want you feeling like you gotta steal anything, girl. What if it wasn't me working today? You trying to go to jail?" Dante says, as he takes the items and leads Sydney over to the counter.

He rings up her food and bags it. He pulls cash out of his pocket and slides it into the register to cover the cost. Dante hands the bag of food to Sydney.

Sydney can't look up at him. She takes the bag without looking him in the eyes. "Thanks," she says in a voice slightly above a whisper.

"What you doing out here stealing, Syd? I know Mrs. V left ya'll some money." Dante sees a sadness in Sydney that pierces him to his core.

"Yea, she did. But she left it in a trust account. I can't get to it without Rita's help and she ain't feeling helpful lately." Sydney chuckles uneasily and scratches her neck.

She can feel the withdrawals kicking in now. It's been days since she could afford to get high.

Dante can tell she's feeling it.

"You know what you need? A distraction," he says as he points to the help wanted sign in the window.

"I can get you a job here. At least until you can work it out with Rita." Dante flashes a nurturing smile.

Truth be told, he's always had a crush on Sydney. He always tried flirting with her, but she never gave him the time of day. Watching her spiral out of control over the last few years broke his heart.

Sydney wants to say no. She's not thrilled about working at a gas station, but she knows he's right. Sitting around the house all day makes it impossible for her to focus on anything besides getting high. Plus, she needs the money.

She gives him a grateful smile and nod.

"Ok, when can I start?" she asks, choking back her tears.

"You can start as soon as you fill this out." Dante reaches over the counter and grabs an application. He hands it to Sydney.

Sheila's heels click and clack as she walks down the hall of the law firm where she works. Her brilliant legal mind mixed with her street smarts have made her a rising star at the majority white law firm. She knows they probably only hired her because they needed a black face on their legal team, but she couldn't care less.

She knows her record of wins in the courtroom speaks to her merit and value on the team. Since she knows she was a diversity hire, she refuses to live up to their expectations of the lazy black woman. She makes sure they see that she's the hardest working junior partner and she's always the last one to leave in the evening.

She's figured out a way to present her arguments around the conference room table with a smile and cool tone, so she doesn't have to be that angry black woman most of the senior attorneys expect her to be. That doesn't stop her from going back to her office, silently screaming and mumbling curse words under her breath behind closed doors.

"Good morning, Mrs. Stone." Her assistant, Corey greets her with a cheerful smile and hands her a stack of papers as Sheila walks past his desk.

"Good morning." Sheila returns his smile as she takes the papers.

She knows he has gossip. He looks around the office discreetly before leaning in closer to her. His thin shoulders shimmy as he lets out his favorite word.

"Girlllll" Corey starts as he purses his lips.

"Tom's car got repossessed this morning!" Corey says as he falls back in his chair and covers his face with a piece of paper from his desk and chuckles quietly.

Sheila doubles over onto Corey's desk as they both laugh.

She hired Corey shortly after the firm hired her. She needed an assistant and she was tired of being the only black face around the office.

"Are you serious?" Sheila says, as she giggles quietly.

"Come here!" She whispers as she motions for Corey to follow her into her office.

Corey rushes into her office and shuts the door behind them.

"Girl, so he comes in this morning and parks in his space in the front. Baby, he rushes past me without speaking, as usual. He doesn't even acknowledge my presence when I say hello to him!" Corey explains.

Sheila motions for him to lower his voice.

"Sorry, girl. But anyway, so while he's in there ordering his assistant around, telling her to get his coffee and pick up his dry cleaning, I see this tow truck pull up outside next to his car. The man gets out and starts hooking up his car, right? So, I rush into Tom's office and try to tell him. He cuts me off as soon as I start talking! Girl, he asks me to go pull all the files for that case he was working on last week. So, I'm thinking, first of all, I'm not your damn assistant! Why do you have your assistant running around doing your personal errands, but you expect me to do the actual work? But I digress." Corey rolls his eyes and lets out an exasperated laugh.

Sheila is amused by how animated he is. He can take the smallest thing and turn it into a hilarious moment.

"So, did you tell the man they were out there towing his car?" Sheila laughs.

"Girl, I politely waited for him to stop talking. Then I said, sure, I'll pull those files for you. I just thought you should know that someone is outside towing your car." Corey collapses onto the ivory sofa in Sheila's office as he tries his best not to laugh too loud.

"Girl, the man jumps up and almost knocks me down, trying to get outside to his car. By the time he got out there, his car was already hooked up to the tow truck. Honey, he was outside screaming at the man, threatening to sue him and everything if he didn't put that damn car down! Baby, the man said fuck you and drove off! Tom's face was so red when he came back in the office. Child, I had to run to the bathroom so I could get myself together. I ain't laughed that hard in so long, girl!" Corey fans himself as he chuckles.

Sheila collapses next to him as they laugh.

"It wouldn't be funny if he wasn't such an asshole!" Sheila says, trying her best to keep her laugh quiet.

Tom is a junior partner at the firm that fights her every chance he gets. He makes no secret about the fact that he thinks she's underqualified. He's never said it directly to her, but the way that he undermines her every chance he gets speaks volumes. Although she's won almost every case that's been put in front of her, he's never liked that she's joined their boy's club. He hates that she's at the same level he is.

He's a brown noser that's fighting to be made senior partner. He recently went through a very messy divorce where his wife took half of everything he had. It's rumored that he also has to pay her a hefty sum each month in alimony and child support.

He so blatantly tries to keep up with the free spending of the senior partners. Tom desperately wants to be seen as one of them. However, the lavish lunches, dinners and trips are catching up to him.

A few months ago, one of the senior partners bought a new luxury Mercedes Benz. It's nearly a hundred-thousand-dollar car. The other senior partners drive cars just as expensive. Tom had to have one. Clearly, he couldn't afford it.

"I feel kinda bad for him, though," Sheila says as she leans her back against the couch.

"He's clearly in trouble. I hate that he's such a jerk. Normally I wouldn't find his situation funny." Sheila tries to empathize.

Corey snatches his head around to make eye contact with her. He cocks his head to the side.

"Girl please! The way that asshole treats you and anyone else that he thinks is beneath him is ridiculous! He deserves to be chopped down to size a bit." Corey clicks his tongue and rolls his eyes as hard as he can.

"Anyway, girl, let's get down to business. I think I found what you're looking for to help your little boyfriend out." Corey taps the paperwork he gave her earlier.

"Did you know that officer was involved in the shooting of an unarmed black man six years ago? The department did a quiet investigation and put him on a paid suspension while they did it! Then they just let him go back to work like it never happened. It never made any real news because the guy was a loner with no real family and only one good friend. So, there was no one to make a real fuss about it. The friend had a criminal background so a few of the officer's friends intimidated him into never talking. But according to the friend that was in the car at the time of the shooting, the officer asked the man for his ID and shot him when he went for it!" Corey shakes his head in disgust.

"He didn't really want to talk about it, but he's a friend of a friend of mine so I set it up and got the story out of him. I think he'll testify if you ask him to." Corey folds his arms with a cocky look on his face.

Sheila stands up as she focuses on the documents. She grips the papers to her chest as she smiles at Corey.

"I'm giving yo ass a raise!" she says as she rushes over and hugs him.

Rita stands outside the door of the condo she once shared with Keith. It's been over a month since she moved out. He invited her over so they could discuss how to get the feds out of their life. Since the office is shut down, they have no way to make money. Keith burns through cash quickly with his addiction and they spent most of their savings last year when they opened their private practice. As much as Rita likes to flaunt her money with expensive clothes and purses, there really isn't much left.

Although they have no money coming in, they're still spending money every month. Rita's living off of her credit cards. She doesn't want to admit it, but it would be easier if she and Keith could makeup and she could move out of the hotel and back into the condo. However, her pride won't allow her to ask him.

Rita pulls out her key to unlock the door, then stops herself. It's rude to just barge in since she's no longer living here. She knocks. Keith opens the door and peers out, smiling. He's looked better. His beard is scruffy and ragged. He's also in desperate need of a haircut. His face is thin, and his eyes are sunken in. The time off work has not been good to him. He looks like shit.

Although he is dressed nicely in a salmon-colored shirt that Rita always loved on him and he's wearing the expensive cologne she bought him.

"Hi, can I come in?" Rita asks, being as nice as she can. Keith steps aside and gestures for her to come in.

"You look beautiful, girl. You're glowing." Keith grins charmingly at her. "Thank you," Rita replies as she walks into the condo and looks around.

She can immediately tell he hasn't cleaned up. It's clear that his things were probably thrown around the apartment and he picked them up five minutes before she got there. The hardwood floors haven't been swept and the coffee table has crumbs on it. She peers into the kitchen and notices the sink full of dishes. Rita rolls her eyes discreetly.

"So, you called me over, right? What are you going to do to fix our situation with the feds?" she says, as she seats herself on the couch.

Keith sits next to her on the sofa. "Well, I've been thinking. They don't have any real evidence against us..." Keith starts.

"Against you, Keith. You mean they have no evidence against you." Rita corrects him but tries not to be too sharp in her tone.

She can feel the anger rising up inside of her, but she tries her best to press it back down. She can't afford to lose it on him, not yet anyway. Keith can sense her rage bubbling just below the surface.

"Ok, you're right. I'm sorry. I did this, I know that." He reaches for her, but she pulls away.

"I have a friend of a friend that works for the DEA. They seriously don't have anything concrete. All they have are suspicions! Baby, they're just digging around. All we have to do is..." Keith explains nervously but is cut off again.

"No, Keith! All you have to do is tell the truth!" Rita stands up and screams in his face.

"You will not compromise my medical license! Do you understand how hard I worked to become a damn doctor? I didn't come from well off, well-educated parents like you did. My parents had nothing to give me, but love and support! Your dad wrote a check and paid for your tuition. I worked my ass off to put my damn self through medical school!" Rita rips her jacket off as she feels herself sweating.

She tries to calm herself. She breathes deeply as she stares at him. "Baby, I can't just..." Keith tries again.

"You can! You can, Keith. If they find something... we're done. We both lose our ability to practice! I opened that damn practice! Me! It was my sweat and my blood that opened it! I did everything! While you sat around and snorted half our fucking life savings up your nose! I used what we had left to open our office. We are broke, Keith! We were just beginning to turn a profit and now our office is closed!" Rita throws her hands up in defeat.

She walks over to the recliner that faces their floor to ceiling window. It overlooks downtown Memphis. She leans forward in the chair and puts her head in her hands. She lets the tears flow freely without trying to stop them.

Keith crosses over to her. He sits on the floor and rests his head on her lap.

"You don't deserve this," he says through his own falling tears.

"I'm sorry I put you through this. I will make it right. I'll just tell them it was all me and that you had absolutely nothing to do with it. If I do time, I'll just do time," Keith says as he lifts her head from her hands.

He wipes away her tears with his hand and kisses her softly on the lips. Rita resists his kiss, then surrenders to it. She pulls him in closer. His strong hands caress her body. Her hands are clenched tightly into fists. She hits him as he kisses her. Her tears are still flowing. Her anger wants to fight him, but the love she still has for him causes her to sink into him. Keith lifts her up. She wraps her legs around his waist. He carries her to their bedroom and lays her on the bed.

Keith tears off her clothes. He licks her neck. Kisses her collar bone and makes his way down to her breasts. He takes his time and gently nibbles and massages them. Rita writhes in pleasure.
He always knew what he was doing in the bedroom. Keith runs his hand down her normally flat tummy. He can feel how it's grown slightly.

The bump causes him to pause.

"It's really in there, huh?" Keith stares at her tummy and smiles.

"Yea, I'm thirteen weeks today." She gives a half-smile as she places her hand over his hand on her stomach.

"I want my family," Keith says, looking into her eyes.

"I need you to move back in. I want to be with my family," he says as he snuggles up next to her, wrapping his arms around her.

"I never wanted to leave, Keith. I had to. Baby, you were out of control. The only way I'm moving back in is if you promise to go to rehab. I mean it this time, Keith." Rita's eyes plead with him.

"You're right. I know, I need help. It's like I can feel everything I have slipping away from me. I promise you I'm gonna do it this time." Keith pulls her in and kisses her.

The sincerity in his eyes is frightening. She's seen it before. He's promised to get clean so many times she's lost count. Somehow, she allows herself to believe him again. As their bodies intertwine, she decides to give Keith and her marriage one last chance.

Two weeks later, Rita sits alone in her hotel room. She and Keith had decided that it's time for her to move back into the condo. Although she knows it's the best thing for them to do financially right now, she is still having nagging doubts. Rita rubs her belly as she thinks.

She takes a sip of her hot tea and rests her head against the back of her chair. The television is on, but she's not watching it. She can't seem to focus on anything right now.

The life she fought so hard for seems to be unraveling right in front of her. Her phone buzzes on the table in front of her.

She picks up the phone and instantly recognizes the number. Rita sighs loudly before she answers it.

"Hello?" she says in a dry tone.

"Dr. Powers. Hi," Agent Thomas's voice on the other end mimics her dry tone.

"I just wanted to touch base with you to see if you've spoken to your husband lately. I know you two are separated now, but we haven't been able to get in touch with him. For some reason he has not returned our calls. We sent an agent to your residence, but no one answered the door. We believe he was in the residence at the time," Agent Thomas says in an accusatory manner.

Rita rolls her eyes. Keith promised her he would handle all of this.

"Well, I did see him a few days ago. He told me that he had plans to reach out to you," Rita replies.

"If that's the case, then why does he seem to be avoiding us? Do you believe your husband has something to hide?" Agent Thomas says sternly.

"Look, he and I have been separated for almost two months now. If you have something to discuss with him, I suggest you do so. I have nothing to do with any of this!" Rita immediately regrets losing her cool.

"Any of what, Dr. Powers?" Agent Thomas asks smugly. "What are...I don't..." Rita stammers.

"You just said, you don't have anything to do with any of this? I'm just asking what you're referring to," Agent Thomas says calmly.

"Please don't do that. You're trying to twist my words around. What I meant is that I have nothing to do with this investigation. I still don't know why we're being singled out! Look, if I speak to Keith, I'll make sure that he calls you. Goodbye!" Rita hangs up the phone and slams it down on the table.

She hops up and paces back and forth around her hotel room. Her heart is racing as her anger mounts. She rushes back to the table and grabs her phone and dials Keith. Her hands tremble as she fights to compose herself.

The call rolls to voicemail. Rita sinks down into her chair.

Her entire body is seething with rage. She trusted him. He told her he would fix this for her. He told her he would go to jail for her if he needed to. Rita can't help but think of how big of a fool she must be to have honestly believed him.

Rita grabs her purse and rushes out of the door. She hops in her car and speeds away. Keith may not have answered his phone, but he can't stop her from driving over to the condo. Rita barrels down the street towards the condo. Her hotel is only about five minutes away.

She doesn't bother parking. She leaves her emergency lights on and storms inside. She pants heavily as she stands outside her condo door. She pounds on the door as hard as she can with her fist.

Keith doesn't answer the door.

She fishes her keys out of her purse and opens the door.

The place is filthy with trash on the floor and old food has been left out on the kitchen counter.

Rita is still panting. She's trying to calm down as she walks into the bedroom looking for Keith.

He's nowhere to be found. Rita is about to turn and leave until she spots something on the nightstand. She moves in closer and feels her heart sink as she realizes what she's looking at. The small glass pipe lay there next to a blackened spoon and a lighter.

She doesn't know why she's so upset. Deep down she knew that he was lying when he told her he was clean. Rita lets her heart break and the tears flow as she walks out of the condo.

Dante peeks at Sydney as she rings up customers. She's been working with him for a few weeks now. He can't take his eyes off her. Her caramel skin glows as she works. She tucks her long curly hair behind one ear as she hands a customer his bag of goods and smiles. Dante hides behind the chip rack pretending to stock it, but really, he's just positioned himself there so he can look at her.

He hasn't found the courage to ask her out yet. He plays it cool day by day but being this close to his childhood crush every day is killing him. He tries to keep it strictly professional. She's been through a lot. He can tell she's doing everything she can to stay sober and he knows she's not ready for a relationship. For now, he plays the role of a supportive friend. He knows that's what she needs right now, so he keeps his feelings to himself.

Dante checks his watch. It's 7:15.

"Hey, Syd." He says, making his way over to her.

He goes behind the counter and whispers in her ear, so the customers won't hear him.

"You better get going. It's almost time for your AA meeting." Dante's been keeping track of her meetings and making sure she goes every day.

"Damn, you're right." Sydney checks the time on her phone.

"I'll finish up here, then head out. It's right down the street." Sydney winks at him and turns around and keeps working.

As Sydney finishes up with the last customer in line, a familiar car pulls up outside. Sydney rolls her eyes, Rita.

"Uh oh, I see your sister's out there. What the hell she want?" Dante asks as he chuckles.

He can tell Rita's presence is irritating Sydney.

"You want to run in the back, and I'll get rid of her?" he offers.

"No, I got it." Sydney sighs as she walks out from behind the counter.

Rita walks into the store. Her keys jingling in her hand as her red-bottomed heels click on the floor.

"Hey, Sydney. Can I talk to you?" Rita asks.

"Sure, I was about to head out though. Can you make it quick?" Sydney walks over to Rita who grabs her arm and leads her to the corner of the store.

"Look, Syd. I'll just say it," Rita starts, her eyes dart around like she's searching for the right words.

Sydney has never known her well-spoken sister to be at a loss for words. She can tell it must be serious.

"I just came to...um..." Rita stammers.

"Look, I came to apologize to you. I shouldn't have refused to help you when you called me last month. I should have just gone with you to get money from the bank. You were right, it's not my money, Mama left it for all of us." Rita breathes deeply as if it pained her to say it.

"Wow, thank you for saying that." Sydney is taken aback by Rita's apology. She can't remember the last time her sister apologized for anything.

"It's cool, Ri. Actually, you were right that day. I mean, yea, I was broke, and I needed to buy food. But, honestly, if you had given me that money, I would have used it to get high. I'm kinda glad you didn't help me. I'm clean now, I'm going to meetings every day, I have a job now." Sydney smiles, proudly.

"Well, that's great." Rita nods her head up and down as she looks around the store. "Yea, Jack mentioned that you were working here."

"So, I guess I'm grateful that you said no. As mad as I was that day, I'm actually glad it happened now." Sydney shrugs.

Rita shifts uncomfortably.

"Good. I'm glad that's behind us. But, hey, I'm happy to go down to the bank with ya'll tomorrow if you want to. I don't want you guys to be struggling when Mama left us all that money," Rita offers.

Sydney's tempted by the offer.

"You know what, I think it's better that I don't get that money right now. I have everything I need. I'm staying in Mama's house and her bills are paid up. I really only need money for food right now and I'm making a little money here. I'm good, Ri." Sydney gives her sister a grateful pat on the shoulder.

"I actually need to head out. My meeting is starting in like twenty minutes." Sydney checks the time on her phone.

"But what's the harm in just putting the money in an account, just in case you need it, Syd? I'll pick you up in the morning and we'll head over to the bank, ok?" Rita presses the issue.

"I just don't think it would be good for me to have access to all that cash right now, Rita. I'm trying to stay clean. I just don't want to go backward. Trust me, I'm good. I have all I need for right now." Sydney shakes her head and waves her hand as if dismissing the idea.

"I do appreciate you coming down here though. I gotta get to my meeting," Sydney says as she tries to walk away.

"Wait, Syd. Just let me take you down there tomorrow. I mean if you want, I'll just keep the money for you until you're ready for it. I got you, it's no problem," Rita urges, almost aggressively. She grabs Sydney's arm before she can walk away.

Sydney turns around and looks at Rita. She's startled by the look in Rita's eyes. Sydney's never seen that look from Rita before. It's desperation.

"Hold up, you need the money, don't you?" Sydney steps back and folds her arms.

"You didn't come here because you felt bad and wanted to apologize. You only apologized because you need me."
Sydney is shocked as the words fall out of her mouth. She never expected to be in this situation with Rita. The shoe is snugly on the other foot now.

"Can you keep your voice down?" Rita tries to pull Sydney back over into the corner of the store.

Sydney snatches away from her.

"You have got to be fucking kidding me! So, instead of just coming out and saying you need money, you come down here and pretend that you're trying to help me? Seriously?" Sydney's voice carries throughout the store.

Rita looks mortified, although there are no customers in the store right now.

Dante pretends to busy himself behind the counter, but he's overheard every word. He keeps his head down and doesn't look at them.

"I'm sorry, ok? I should I have just been honest with you. But I did mean what I said. I have felt bad about not helping you that day." Rita fights through her humiliation.

"See, now I don't believe it. Your apology doesn't mean shit now cause you lied first! It feels like you're just saying it, so I'll help you. Why shouldn't I just leave your ass high and dry like you did me?" Sydney asks furiously.

"I know, and you have every right to do it. But I really was genuinely concerned that you would overdose and kill yourself, Syd. If you had been clean, I never would have turned you down," Rita says firmly.

Sydney rolls her eyes and lets out an annoyed sigh.

"So, what's going on? What you need the money for?" Sydney says, sucking her teeth loudly as she waits for a response.

"We're having some issues with our practice. We had to close down for a little while." Rita is near tears as she answers.

"What kind of problems? Ya'll ain't got no patients coming in? What?" Sydney presses. "It's just, um. We're um... being audited," Rita lies.

"It happens to doctor's offices all the time. But we just had to close the office while they do it. it's completely normal." Rita tries to sound confident.

"Nah, something ain't right about that. If it's so normal, why would they make you shut the office down while they do it?" Sydney clicks her tongue and laughs to herself.

"I bet you it's got something to do with Keith, don't it? They investigatin' him, huh?" Sydney smiles, she's sure she's guessed correctly.

"Damn! Ok, Syd. Yes! Alright? The DEA has the office shut down because of Keith." Rita lets a tear fall.

"I know I've been hard on you. But most of that was about him. I took so much of the anger I had for him out on you. It wasn't fair to you, Syd. I'm sorry." Rita can't look at her sister.

Sydney sees the brokenness on her sister's face.

"Thank you for saying that. I know I've put the family through a lot. I've been messed up for a long time, but I'm seriously trying to get my shit together now. All I've ever wanted was to get some support from my big sister. But you have belittled me and laughed at my struggle the whole time I was going through it." Sydney moves in closer to Rita.

"I'm not gonna do that to you. I'll meet you at the bank tomorrow. Text me the time you wanna meet," Sydney says. She turns and gives a wave to Dante as she walks out of the store.

Jack was released from jail on bond a week ago. The judge agreed to let him out while the police officer who killed Mrs. Virginia's case plays out in court. Sheila had to fight hard for that.

They wanted to keep Jack in jail until his court date, which hadn't even been set yet. With the way the legal system drags its feet, who knows how long he would have had to sit in there?

Sheila came up with the brilliant idea to press criminal charges against the officer. She alleged that he was harassing the family of the woman he killed when he showed up to her funeral. Sheila is also pushing for a homicide charge. She requested that the officer face a jury. He shouldn't only have an internal affairs investigation; we all know how that will turn out.

When they go to court, she'll bring up his previous investigation relating to the death of Antwon Hinds, the unarmed man he killed a few years ago. The friend that witnessed the whole thing is finally ready to testify.

Jack walks into the convenience store where Sydney has been working for the last few weeks.

Dante gives a smile and a quick up nod.

"Jack-Jack, what's up?" Dante laughs as he reaches over and cooly shakes his hand.

"What's up, D? Now, you know Syd is the only one to get away with calling me that." Jack laughs as he greets Dante.

"So, I guess you're not hiding out anymore?" Dante jokes.

"Nah, I had to get out of the house. I was just sitting around driving myself crazy," Jack says as he looks around the store.

"You seen Syd?" Jack asks, concerned.

"I was gon ask you the same thing. She ain't been to work in a couple days. I've been covering for her, but I can't do that much longer," Dante admits.

"Damn, I've been trying to call her, but she ain't been answering the phone. She won't even call me back. The only time she do that is when she using." Jack shakes his head.

"Yea, I was afraid of that. I was bout to swing by your mom's house when I get off work," Dante says.

"Don't bother. I just left there. She wasn't home." Jack rubs his bald head.

"Look, just call me if you see her. But don't tell her I stopped by. She already feels like the family is always checking up on her. She thinks everyone expects her to fail." Jack sighs, he turns and walks out of the store.

Dante watches Jack drive away then drops his head and exhales deeply. He walks over to the old wooden door behind the register and opens it.

Sydney is curled up on a worn sofa in the employee breakroom. She's shivering and sweating. Dante wipes her forehead with a moist towel.

He sits next to her on the sofa and rubs her back as she shakes.

"He's gone," Dante says reassuringly.

"I'm sorry...I tried ...I tried..." Sydney cries as she shivers.

"It's ok, Syd. You're ok. I know you tried your best. I didn't tell him nothin about the relapse. But once you feel better, I think you should call him. You know Jack, he's worried about you." Dante wipes her face with the moist towel.

"I will. I'll call him." Sydney begins heaving.

She leans over a trash can next to the sofa and up chucks. When she's finished, Dante wipes her mouth and gives a sip of water.

He's been taking care of Sydney for two days. He got concerned when she didn't show up for work three days in a row. He went by her house and found her passed out on the floor. She had drugs all over the living room table.

She told him it started after she helped Rita get money out of the trust account. Turns out she was right, having all that cash in hand was a trigger for her. She got high again a couple of days after she got the money.

Dante watches as Sydney falls asleep. Taking care of her has only made his feelings grow stronger. He knows he's in love with her but telling her that is not an option right now. He doesn't want to scare her away or put too much on her while she's going through the hardest moments of her life.

"Hey, is anybody working here?!" Dante hears a customer shout from the front of the store.

Dante covers Sydney with a blanket and kisses her forehead before heading back up front.

Sheila flies into her neighborhood, whipping around the corner and swerving as she zips down the street to her house.

There's a press conference today at 5 o'clock. It's 5:13. The police department is announcing the results of the investigation against Mrs. Virginia's killer.

Sheila just got word from one friend about the results of the investigation. As soon as she found out she rushed out of the office so she could be with Jack when he watched the press conference.

Sheila glides her car quickly into her garage and closes the garage door. She hops out of the car without grabbing her purse or briefcase. She leaves her car door slightly opened as she runs into the house. It's 5:18.

The sound of smashing glass stops her in tracks. She's panting heavily. She walks around the corner into the living room and sees Jack standing over her flat-screen television. The television lies smashed on the living room floor. Jack's chest heaves up and down as he stands there, fists clenched and his jaw tight. He wears a white tank top and basketball shorts.

"They cleared him. They're dropping the charges against that mother fucker!" Jack says, almost growling at her.

"Baby, I'm so sorry. I tried to get here before you found out." Sheila walks over to him and tries to put her arms around him.

Jack snatches away from her. He stomps over to the front door and punches a hole in the wall near the door. He yanks the door open and walks out, slamming it behind him.

Sheila feels herself crumbling from the inside out. She fights to catch her breath. Every part of her wants to follow Jack, but she knows there's nothing she can say to make it better. She feels her heart being ripped from her chest while she watches through the window as he walks away.

Sydney sits on the floor next to her mother's favorite chair. Her head rests on the worn and crackled leather. The seat is wet with her tears.

Two hours ago, she watched the press conference as the police department announced that Officer Avery, the man who killed her mother, would not be charged in her death.

Her eyes are fixed on the coffee table. A small bag of white powder rests there taunting her. She ran out of the house and bought it as soon as she heard the verdict. When she got home, she collapsed onto the floor and hasn't been able to move since. Her heart aches as she wraps her arms around the chair where her mother once sat.

Her mind drifts back to the days when she sat between Virginia's legs getting her hair braided. She smiles and swats away her tears as she recalls being popped with the comb whenever she moved around too much.
The jingling of keys in the front door causes her to jump to her feet. She grabs the small plastic bag from the coffee table and shoves it into her pocket.

Rita pushes through the door. She stands in the doorway, her eyes red and swollen. Sydney can see the tracks of her tears carving a path through her makeup. Sydney rushes over to her sister and wraps her arms around her. The pair share a genuine hug for the first time in more years than either of them can remember.

They hold each other as the tears stream down; neither of them wants to let go.

"I guess I didn't get an invite to the party," Jack says as he stands in the doorway watching them.

Sydney and Rita wear matching pained grins as they motion for him to come in. Jack drapes his arms around his sisters.

"It's crazy that we couldn't get past our own bull shit and get together while mama was alive. I hate that she had to die in order for us to be able to do this," Jack says.

Rita folds her arms and sighs.

"I know most of it had to do with my judgmental ass. All I've been thinking about lately is how much time I spend acting like I'm perfect, and like my life is perfect. Well, it's not," Rita says as she sits down in her mother's chair.

"We need to air some shit out. Let me start. First of all, I'm pregnant. My husband is a doctor that happens to be addicted to drugs. Because of him, our practice is under investigation and has been shut down indefinitely. Also, I'm broke! Every dime I have is tied up in that practice, so I have no way of making money right now; and my medical license is suspended until they finish the investigation." Rita shrugs her shoulders as she leans back in the chair and props her feet up on the coffee table.

"Well, damn!" Jack says as he and Sydney fall into each other as they howl with laughter. Sydney sits on the arm of the chair and hugs Rita.

"Girl, I knew you were going through some shit, but I didn't know it was all that." Sydney smiles as she hugs her.

"Listen, I'm telling ya'll all of this because I'm done hiding. I feel like I've been this goody two shoes version of myself since I was a kid. I'm tired of feeling like I have to be the perfect one, or the strong one. I'm done. I'm not hiding my mistakes or my failures anymore. And I'm sorry that I have been making both of you feel bad for your mistakes. Mama used to always say that life has a way of humbling you. She was right," Rita admits as she squeezes her sister.

"Now, let me admit something else. I'm hungry! I think this baby wants some pizza." She laughs as she pulls out her phone to call in the order.

Later, the trio eat and snort with laughter as they remember their parents and berate each other with embarrassing stories of their childhood.

"Who is that?" Jack asks as he notices a shadow outside the window.

As they all quiet down, they hear voices chanting outside. It's hard to make out what's being said, but they all seem to be saying the same thing.

Jack's jaw drops as he peeks out of the window.

"Who is it?" Sydney asks hopping up and running to the window. She gasps at what she sees there.

With Jack and Sydney blocking the front window, Rita walks over to the door and peers out of the peephole.

There are two women dressed in black and white t-shirts standing on the front porch. Behind them, the entire front yard and the street in front of the house is overflowing with people. Mostly young black people with a few other ethnicities sprinkled amongst the crowd.

Rita can now read their t-shirts: Black Lives Matter.

Jack nudges Rita gently out of the way and opens the door.

"Excuse me, sir," a beautiful bronze-skinned woman on the porch says politely. Her long- braided hair is tossed over one shoulder.

"We meant no disrespect by showing up to your home unannounced. But we were outraged by the press conference today. We wanted to come here and show our support."

"Her life mattered! Her life mattered!" a young man in the crowd yells loudly.

The group quickly follows suit, and within seconds, everyone is rhythmically chanting with raised fists, "Her life mattered!"

Jack, Sydney and Rita stand together on the front porch as the crowd yells.

Sydney sits on the steps of the porch as she breaks down in tears. She pictures how proud her mother would be to see the community come together in this overwhelming show of love and support.

Rita sits next to her and puts her arm around her. Jack seats himself on the step next to them.

The crowd seems to be growing by the second. Soon, news crews and police officers show up.

A tall blonde woman dressed in an expensive blue suit and heels makes her way to the front of the crowd with a cameraman following closely behind her.

She walks over to them and holds a microphone in their face.

"What do you all have to say about the protesters showing up here tonight?" she asks.

Sydney grabs the microphone and leaps to her feet.

"Her name was Virginia Johnson. She was our mother. I don't even have words to describe how much we loved her. Tonight, the police officer that murdered her was cleared of all charges! You want to know what I have to say about that? I say her life mattered! *Her life mattered!* HER LIFE MATTERED!" Sydney screams and pumps her frail fist.

Rita and Jack stand up and join their sister's chant. The crowd chants along, louder and stronger than ever.

"Her life mattered!"

CHAPTER FIVE

R ita stands in the living room of the condo she once shared with Keith. This is the third time she's popped up here. There's still no so sign of him. He hasn't answered her calls or texts for the last few weeks. What's worse is that Agent Thomas is still breathing down her neck.

Rita's phone buzzes from inside her purse. She knows who it is before she looks at the phone.

"He's not here," Rita says as she answers the call. "What a surprise, Dr. Powers," Agent Thomas says.
She and her partners have been camping outside of the condo for days now trying to ambush Keith.

"Look, we have enough evidence to charge your husband in this matter. If you don't help us find him, we may have to charge you with obstruction of justice. I'm getting very impatient, Doctor," the agent says aggressively.

"Damn it, I told you! I have no idea where he is. I'm starting to think that wherever he is, he's hiding from me too! What do you expect me to do?" Rita stomps her foot as she screams into the phone.

"You need to figure something out, Rita! Because wherever he is, he seems to be hiding strategically. He's also smart enough not to be using his cell phone or his credit cards. Your husband has vanished and left you holding the bag here! Are you willing to go to jail for him?" the Agent says raising her voice.

Rita tears up as she touches her belly.

"I told you. I don't know where he is. She says in almost a whimper.

"Look, I believe you, and I have a good feeling you're innocent in all of this. We combed through everything and we couldn't find a shred of evidence against you. You know, there is a way that you can help us," Agent Thomas responds.

"I don't know what else I can do," Rita says.

The phone disconnects. Rita stares at her phone perplexed. She hears a knock at the door. Rita opens the door and finds herself face to face with Agent Thomas.

"There's one thing you can do. When he reaches out to you, and I know he will. I want you to wear this." She holds up a thin wire with a small microphone attached.

"If you can get him to admit that he stole the pharmaceutical samples and that he committed the prescription fraud, we'll clear your name in all of this. I'll make sure your license is restored and I'll get your practice opened as soon as possible. Of course, this means Keith is going to jail." Agent Thomas admits with a slight sincerity in her voice.

Rita scoffs.

"I can't... I can't do that to him. How do you expect me to do something like that? He's my husband. I can't do it," she says as she starts to break down.

"After everything he has put you through, you're still protecting him?" Agent Thomas asks.

Rita fights to compose herself. She bites her lip as she tries to stop the tears. She curses Keith silently.

"I'll need time to think it over," she says.

"Ok, but you're running out of options. I'll be in touch," the Agent says as she walks out.

Sydney and Dante sit in his car outside of the police station.

"Are you sure this is the best thing for you to be doing right now?" Dante asks. "Yes, this is exactly what I need right now." Sydney smiles at him.

"You know I'm just trying to look out for you. I don't want you to stress yourself out, Syd." Dante's puppy dog eyes beg Sydney to reconsider.

"D, thank you for looking out for me. You have been so supportive of me. But trust me, I need this. I need something to keep my mind occupied." Sydney wraps her arms around Dante.

Dante breathes her in as she hugs him.
She smells like shea butter and lavender flowers.

Dante must admit she's been looking better and better every day lately. This might help her stay clean.

A tap on the window startles them.

Two of the women from the protest at Mrs. Virginia's house stand outside of the car.

Sydney smiles and hops out of the car. She greets them both warmly. One of them hands Sydney a large rolled poster.

"We finally got all of the posters in!" Tiffany, a light-skinned woman with a curly afro says excitedly.
Tiffany and Sade hold up the poster and unroll it. It's about two feet long.

The poster shows a regal photo of Mrs. Virginia next to the words: I stand for Virginia Johnson.

"Do you like it?" Sade, the cute, slightly chubby, bronze-skinned girl asks. Her perfect white teeth gleam as she smiles.

Sydney is awestruck as she stares at the photo of her mother. She tries to speak, but her mouth doesn't move.

"You like it, right? Girl, I hope you do cause we have about twenty of these and we have t- shirts!" Tiffany says nervously.

Tiffany and Sade look at each other as Sydney stares at the poster silently. "Damn, I was afraid it was too much," Sade says.

"No, I love it." Sydney finally forces the words out.

"It's perfect." Sydney holds onto Dante as she grins up at him with tears in her eyes. Dante holds her tightly and kisses her forehead.

"They're here!" Tiffany points as about thirty young black men and women walk over to them.

They're all wearing t-shirts that bear Virginia's face and are holding signs. Sydney and Dante grab t-shirts from Sade and throw them on over their clothes. They set up camp across the street from the precinct.

Sydney grabs a bullhorn from Tiffany. They spread out across the sidewalk, locking arms and forming a human chain. A few stand behind the line on top of their cars holding up the signs.

Police officers pour out of the building. The officers watch the group closely from across the street as they stand there.

Sydney was careful to obtain a permit before they got there, so the officers have no right to make them leave.

Starting with the first person at the end of the line, they chant one by one: I stand for Virginia Johnson!

Tears pour down Sydney's face as she yells with a shaking voice, "I stand for Virginia Johnson", as her turn comes.

Dante breaks down in tears as he shouts, "I stand for Virginia Johnson!" right after Sydney.

Sydney spots Officer Avery in the sea of police officers across the street. His face is blood red as he watches the protest. Sydney sees what looks like remorse on his face as he turns and walks back into the building.

Half an hour into the chanting and raised fists, three officers walk slowly across the street and cautiously approach the group.

The media showed up ten minutes ago and there are at least fifteen cellphone cameras pointed at them. The officers are primed to do whatever they can to make the protesters leave with no incidents.

Sydney and the protesters bead with sweat as the hot Memphis sun beams down on them. Their screams intensify as the officers approach.

A tall, thin black officer leads as two muscular white officers follow him closely.

"We, um, respect your right to protest lawfully," the tall, black officer says as if he memorized a script before he came out.

"What can we do to help resolve this peacefully?" he continues.

The white officers stand stiffly behind him as they watch the crowd uneasily. Their hands rest on their waists near their guns.

"We call for Officer Avery's immediate termination!" Sydney yells confidently into the bullhorn.

The group cheers behind her. The news cameras swarm around her as she talks.

"We've also done research on this precinct, there are two other officers who were involved in the questionable killing of unarmed black and brown men! With that being said, we also call for the immediate termination of Officer Piedmont and Officer Freeman! They were also given a slap on the wrist and a paid suspension after they murdered innocent men! This must stop! We are here today not only to protest the killing of my mother, but all of the lives that have been lost at the hands of police officers who shoot first and ask questions later! All of the officers who would rather kill someone than try to deescalate the situation. We are here not to say that our lives are more important than anyone else's. We are here to simply say that our lives matter! Black lives matter!" Sydney shouts into the bullhorn.

The crowd erupts in thunderous cheers and applause. The officers look around nervously as the crowd cheers.

"We have heard your requests and I will take these matters to our captain for a full review. Thank you." the black officer says as he turns and hurriedly walks back across the street.

News anchors fight each other to interview Sydney.

After the protest dies down, Dante walks Sydney to the car. He couldn't keep his eyes off of her as she shouted in the protest. Her strength is mesmerizing. She's never looked more beautiful to him. He tries not to stare, but he's finding it almost impossible.

Sydney catches his eye as he stares lovingly at her. She wraps her arms around him and rests her head on his chest. She looks up at him as she holds him. Her eyes seem to shine brightly as she smiles up at him.

As the sun sets, Dante takes his chance. He leans down and kisses her passionately as he pulls her into him. Sydney's stomach flips as she grabs his long dreads in her hands. She can't deny that she's been wanting this for a while now but was afraid that he only saw her as a pathetic junkie.

Dante pushes her against the car as he kisses her. Sydney runs her hands across his broad shoulders.

"You have no idea how long I've been wanting to do that," he says as he stares into her eyes.

"Probably about as long as I've been waiting for you to do it."
Sydney chuckles. "I told you they were together!" Sade says to
Tiffany as they walk by and wave.

Sydney and Dante fall into each other as they laugh and wave
them off.

Rita sits alone in her car in the parking lot of her hotel.

"You arrogant, selfish son of a bitch!" Rita screams into her phone
as she vents to Keith's voicemail.

She's been looking everywhere for him but still can't seem to find
him. Agent Thomas told her that if they don't hear from him by
tomorrow, they'll put a warrant out for his arrest.

"I feel like such an idiot. You seriously had me convinced that you
would turn yourself in and make this right. You have never been
able to think about anyone but yourself," Rita says in a dry tone.

"I think what hurts me more than anything, is that when
everything you did hit the fan, you left me holding the bag. You
screwed up my business, you compromised my medical license and
then you disappeared. What's worse, you didn't even think to take
me with you. You left me here to clean up your mess." Rita sobs
into her cell phone.

A rage burns inside her as she cries.

"You are a spineless piece of shit. I have always known that about you. You're soft just like your mama raised you to be! You have never had to work for anything! You couldn't even get yourself into medical school, your daddy had to write a check to get you in! What kind of man would run and leave his wife to go down for something he did? That's just who you are and that's who you have always been, and I am a fucking moron for not realizing it sooner." Rita hangs up the phone and tosses it on the passenger seat.

Her heart pounds as she breathes heavily, trying to catch her breath. Her eyes are red and swollen. Tears stain her cheeks.

She rests her head on the seat and closes her eyes as she inhales and exhales deeply. Her phone rings. She quickly sits up and snatches it from the seat.

It's Agent Thomas.

"Look, I still don't know where he is," she answers, annoyed by the call.

"No, that's not why I'm calling. We actually found him," Agent Thomas says calmly.

"You did? Oh, my God! Well, that's great. I have been driving myself crazy looking for him." Rita breathes a sigh of relief.

"Yes, he's here. We actually need you to come down here," the Agent says. "Where? To the police station?" Rita asks.

"No, actually we need you to come to Methodist Hospital. We need you to get here as soon as you can," Agent Thomas says.

"Hospital? Is he ok?" Rita feels her heart sink as if she already knows the answer.

"You'll want to get here as soon as possible," Agent Thomas says before hanging up the phone.

Half an hour later, Rita walks into Methodist Hospital in downtown Memphis.

Her body is numb as her red-bottomed heels click clack down the hallway. She can't even remember how she got here. Her body was on autopilot as she drove.

"Rita!" Jack calls to her as he hops up out of a waiting room chair.

Rita texted him and Sydney and begged them to meet her there. Sydney rushes in the doorway with Dante trotting behind her. She grabs Rita who looks like she's in shock.

"Ri? You ok? What's going on?" Sydney asks, as she pats her sister's face. "Is the baby ok?" Jack asks as he puts his arm around her.

"He's gone," Rita replies as she tries to get her eyes to focus on her sister and brother. "Who's gone? Keith? Where did he go?" Sydney asks.

"He died." Rita eeks the words out.

"The agent handling our case called and told me they finally found him. She told me to meet her here," Rita explains.

"Did she say he died? Maybe he's just in the hospital. How do you know he died?" Jack replies.

Agent Thomas walks around the corner and stops in her tracks when she sees Rita.

"She didn't have to say it." Rita locks eyes with Agent Thomas, who takes off her FBI cap and smooths her hair back.

She walks toward Rita.

"He overdosed?" Rita asks through a shaking voice.

"You'll have to identify him before I confirm that," the Agent says.

"I know it's him. But I would like to see him," Rita says, as her eyes swell with tears.

Jack grabs the garbage can from the back of the house and drags it around to the front. He's been at his mother's house with Rita and Sydney since yesterday. Keith was laid to rest yesterday as well.

Rita has been staying here with Sydney ever since the night they found Keith dead in his car with a needle hanging out of his arm. She's mostly been staring at the television and stuffing her face with anything she can get. She honestly hasn't cried much at all.

Jack thought for sure she would break down yesterday at the funeral. She just sat there, stiff as a board wearing an expensive black pantsuit and dark black shades.

Jack and Sydney kept a close eye on her throughout the funeral and the repast. They were ready to jump in to offer emotional support if she broke down while talking to Keith's family and friends.

She never did.

Every now and again they would see a single tear escape the bottom of her sunglasses, but she would wipe it away as quickly as it came.

She was stoic and gracious as she spoke to everyone and received their sympathies.

After everyone had gone, she went into her room, shut the door and stayed there for the rest of the night. They tried knocking on the door, but she refused to open it. She let them know that she was ok and just needed time alone in a weak tone.

Sydney slept on the couch just in case she ever came out and wanted to talk.

Around one o'clock in the morning, Sydney woke up to the sound of Rita hunting for food in the fridge. Before Sydney could get up, Rita quickly scurried back into her room with an arm full of food and shut the door.

Today has been more of the same.

Jack drags the garbage can down the driveway toward the curb. He notices a man sitting in a parked car across the street.

As Jack makes his way to the curb, the man gets out of the car and crosses.

Jack positions the trash can on the curb and watches carefully as the man approaches him. Jack seethes with rage as he realizes who it is.

Officer Avery steps onto the curb and holds up his hands as if to show he has no weapon.

Jack's fists instinctively ball up as he blinks, slowly trying to restrain himself from hurting the man again.

"I know this is stupid, me showing up here like this," the officer says, his voice shaking.

"You have got to be out of your fucking mind," Jack says in a grunt through gritted teeth.

"Please hear me out. I didn't come to cause you or your family any more trouble." the officer says, as he shifts uncomfortably.

"Listen, I wanted to let you know, I'm not a racist. I don't hate black people," Avery says almost mumbling. His eyes shift back and forth from his feet to Jack.

"You kill my mama, then you show up here to tell me you're not a racist?" Jack asks in disbelief.

Everything inside him wants to grab and finish what he started at the funeral.

"No, no! I didn't come here for that; I don't know why I started with that." Avery hits himself in the head.

"I'm a veteran. I have PTSD. Sometimes I can get triggered in high-pressure situations. I just wanted you to know that I didn't kill her on purpose..." Avery says shakily.

Jack yanks the man by his collar and slams him to the ground.

"So, you came here to give me some bullshit excuse for why you shot my mama?" Jack yells as he pins Avery to the sidewalk.

"No, I... I didn't!" The officer struggles as he's pinned down on his back.

"You're on my property, bitch. I could kill you and tell them it was self-defense!" Jack wraps his hands around Avery's neck.

"I dropped the charges!" Avery squeaks out as Jack's grip tightens around his neck. Jack stares at him in shock.

"What?" Jack responds.

"I told them that I provoked you. I had no right to show up to your mother's funeral. I got them to drop the charges against you." Avery croaks out the words through Jack's grip around his neck.

Jack stands up, leaving Officer Avery to pick himself up off of the ground.

"It's already done. As soon as I got word that the charges would be dismissed, I just drove straight here so I could tell you and your family. I wanted to apologize for everything I've put your family through." Officer Avery extends his hand to Jack.

Jack slaps the hand away.

"Fuck you! So, is that supposed to bring our mama back?" Jack asks furiously.

"No, it could never bring her back. It's the only thing I could think of to try to make things better. I know this won't make it right, but... maybe I can make it better." Avery's eyes shift to his shoes again.

"You can't make this right and you can't make it better. Whatever the hell that means. You don't get to feel better about what you did! You don't get to make it up to us! My mama is dead, and you killed her!" Jack screams.

"I... I know. I just..." Tears stream down Avery's face.

"And I couldn't give a shit about your tears! I hope this haunts you for the rest of your life! I want you to die knowing that you murdered her!" Jack's voice trembles as his own tears flow.

Rita and Sydney step out onto the porch as they hear the commotion. Officer Avery looks at them all. Their eyes feel like daggers in his soul. Avery turns and walks back across the street. He sees the neighbors staring angrily at him as he slowly gets into his car and drives away.

It's been a month since Keith's death. Rita still can't bring herself to move back into the condo she once shared with him.

She has, however, moved out of the hotel.

Living in her mother's home with Sydney is giving her a comfort she never expected to feel.

Sydney has crafted a delicate balance of checking on Rita yet giving her the space, she needs to grieve.

Watching Sydney as she balances her sobriety, working at the store with Dante, and working with her Black Lives Matter group at night leaves Rita speechless.

Sydney is picking up the pieces of her life and becoming an actual grown-up for the first time at twenty-eight years old.

Rita never thought she would feel this way, but she's actually proud of her sister. Three hard knocks on the front door snap Rita back into consciousness.

She had drifted off to sleep on the couch in the living room. It's been hard finding sleep in her room at night. Every time she closes her eyes, she sees Keith's face. When she does finally fall asleep nightmares of him overdosing in his car, as she pounds on the car window to save him, shock her awake.

Rita squints through the peephole before opening the door.

"I thought I'd find you here," Agent Thomas says with a half-smile.

"I checked the condo and your hotel. You're hard to find these days," she says. Her tone much softer than it was in previous visits.

"Well, you found me. What can I do for you?" Rita asks flatly. She doesn't have the energy for insincere pleasantries.

"May I come in?" Thomas asks.

"I'll come out. I could use a little sunshine anyway," Rita says, as she steps out onto the porch closing the door behind her.

"I just came to tell you that we've closed the case. Your medical license is no longer suspended, and you can resume business at your practice." Agent Thomas blurts the words out, picking up on Rita's tone.

Rita feels her heart skip a beat. "Really? It's over?" She asks. "The case is closed. If I'm being honest, we never suspected that you had any involvement in any of it. Our entire investigation was centered around Keith. It was really his misconduct that triggered the whole thing. But since the two of you shared the business, we had to investigate you too. I didn't find one shred of evidence that you were involved," Thomas says with a shrug.

"Well... I'm glad everything is cleared up now." Tears begin to flow down Rita's cheeks. She tries to blink them away, but it's no use. Her knees buckle, causing her to sit on the top porch step.

She weeps as she rubs her swollen belly. She can feel her baby fluttering around inside her.

"So, what are you having?" Thomas asks as she motions toward Rita's belly.

"It's a boy. His name is Keith. He always wanted boy," Rita responds through her tears.

"Keith. That's a good name. I like it," Thomas says with a half-smile.

"Well, I'm gonna head out. I just wanted to give you the news," Agent Thomas says, as she walks down the old wooden porch steps and heads over to her car.

She stops and turns back toward Rita.

"For what it's worth, I'm really sorry about your husband. None of us wanted it to end like this." the Agent says sincerely.

"Thank you. But honestly, I knew it was coming. I don't think he was strong enough to quit. He was getting more and more out of control. I always knew it would end badly. I was always afraid that he was either going to jail or I'd find him dead on the bathroom floor. Is it wrong that I have more peace now that he's gone?" Rita says in a low tone."

"No, it's not. Peace is peace. Sometimes we find it in strange ways. What's important is that you have it. Try to hang onto it."

Agent Thomas gives a quick wave as she gets in her car.

As Rita watches her drive away, she feels a piece of the heaviness she's been carrying on her shoulders gently lift off of her.

She inhales slowly and deeply. As she exhales, she feels a bit of the pain inside of her release. It feels good, so she does it again. She inhales deeply and pushes the air out of her mouth.

She remembers how her mother used to sit on the front porch during the summer months and feel the evening breeze on her skin as she sipped a glass of sun tea.

Virginia would close her eyes and breathe deeply.

Whenever Rita would ask her mom what she was doing, she would always say, "Child, I'm just sittin' here blowin'."

It was an old country saying and Rita never knew what it meant. She always laughed when her mother said it.

But right now, at this moment, she knows what her mother must have meant and the peace she must have felt to just sit there and blow.

Jack jumps up off of the couch and paces back and forth in the living room as he waits for Sheila to come into the house.

He heard the garage door open a few moments ago. He's been waiting for her to get home all day.

Sheila walks in and kicks her heels off near the door.

Jack rushes over to her and scoops her up in his arms. He kisses her as he twirls her around before putting her back down.

Sheila squeals and giggles. She playfully punches his arm once he puts her down.

"Boy! What is going on with you?" she laughs.

Jack rushes over to the coffee table and picks up a manila folder and hands it to her proudly. She takes the envelope and opens it.

"You passed! Baby, you passed!" Sheila drops the envelope and jumps on Jack wrapping her legs around his waist as she hugs him.

A few weeks after Officer Avery dropped the charges against Jack, he decided it was time to figure out what he wanted to do with his life. He needed a career. A friend of his started selling real estate a few years ago and convinced Jack he could do it too.

Jack started taking classes a month and a half ago. He's been staying up nights studying and preparing for his final test.

Today, he found out that he passed his classes and is now a licensed real estate broker.

"I'm so proud of you." Sheila smiles at him as she hugs him.

"Thank you for believing in me, baby. Oh, and I didn't tell you the best part. My boy Fred got me a job at his real estate company. Plus, Rita wants me to help her sell her condo. She's thinking about buying a house. She wants a fresh start, since Keith passed away. I'm already making money, boo!" Jack says excitedly.

I figure I'll work with Fred for a year or so while I learn the business, then I'll open my own real estate company." Jack smiles broadly.

"Oooh, I am loving this ambitious side of you." Sheila wraps her arms around his waist and kisses him passionately.

"Oh, you like that, huh?" Jack flirts.

"Yes sir, I do." Sheila takes off her blazer then reaches behind her and unzips her skirt, letting it fall to the floor.

She takes off her top and places her hands on her curvaceous hips as she stands there in her black lace bra and matching panties.

She grabs Jack by his belt and leads him into her bedroom.

After they make love, the pair lay side by side on the bed. Their bodies glisten with sweat. Sheila is still tingling as she lays her head on Jack's chest.

Jack reaches over and slaps her on the butt as she stretches her leg around his waist. Sheila gently bites his chest.

"I wanted to tell you something before you see it on the news or something," she says awkwardly.

"Tell me what?" Jack says as he sits up slowly.

"Well, before I left work today, my contact at the police station called me," Sheila continues. "Yea, and what happened?" Jack asks.

"Well, you know your sister and the Black Lives Matter people have been outside of the police station protesting every week. I heard that cop hasn't been handling it that well. He resigned today," Sheila says as she looks at Jack.

"So, he quit? They didn't fire him?" Jack snaps.

"My contact is pretty sure he quit. She thinks he had some kind of breakdown. He seemed pretty unstable," Sheila explains.

"I know the motherfucker is unstable! They should have fired his ass! The bastard told me he had PTSD before he even killed my mama!" Jack is now pacing around the room, naked as he rants.

Sheila bounces out of bed and walks over to him.

"Baby, I know. And if you want me to, I can have my firm file charges against them for having him working the streets with a weapon; while he admittedly had a mental illness. I'm almost positive that they were aware that he had it. But until you're ready to do that, there's really nothing we can do right now. I'm just happy to hear he's off the police force for now." Sheila says.

Jack sits on the edge of the bed.

"Yea, I guess I can just be happy about that." He shakes his head still unsatisfied.

"I'll talk to Syd and Rita. We'll see if they want to go after the police station for keeping him on the force. I don't want to do it if they're happy about him quitting," Jack says before walking into the bathroom and shutting the door behind him.

Sydney locks the front door of the store. She flips over the sign on the door that reads "Open" to make sure it now says "Closed."

She makes her way to the back of the store where Dante sits counting down the registers.

"Alright, girl, let's get up out of here," he says winking at her.

"Yes, please. I'm starving. You want to pick up a pizza on the way home?" Sydney asks sweetly.

"That'll work. Call it in. I'll be done in a minute," Dante says as he hurries to finish up.

Sydney pulls her cell phone out of her pocket. As she pulls it out, a folded white envelope falls to the floor.

She can't believe she forgot it was in her pocket. "What's that?" Dante asks.

Sydney picks it up and unfolds it. She tries to press out the creases with her hands before she gives it to him.

Dante takes the envelope and opens it. He pulls out a check made out to him, for five million dollars. It's the check Mrs. Virginia's lawyer sent him months earlier.

The sight of it flusters him.

Sydney sees the same pain on his face she saw when he gave the check back to her months ago.

"Ok, ok, wait." she says as she sits next to him.

"I can't... I told you I can't..." Dante shakes his head "no" as he tries to hand it back to her.

"Yes, you can. She wanted you to have it. Just think about it for a moment. She told me she would never have won that money if it weren't for you. You bought her the ticket!" Sydney explains.

"And then I got her killed!" Dante jumps up and tries to walk out, but Sydney grabs him.

"Damn it, I told you that wasn't your fault! That punk ass police officer should never have pulled a gun on you! He did this, not you!" she says as she grabs his face and wipes away his tears.

"But I made him mad. I was being an asshole to that cop. He was trying to shoot me, not her! I can't take money knowing that your family blames me for her death!" Dante says as he tries to hand her the check, but she won't take it.

"You know who gave me this? Rita. She found this today and she gave it to me. She told me to give it to you. She was the only person who blamed you and she let it go! She was just angry, babe. But she wants you to have it now. She knows how important it was to Mama." Sydney hugs him and kisses his cheek.

"Please take it," she pleads as she hugs him.

Dante remembers the rage in Rita's eyes the day he came over after Mrs. Virginia's funeral. He's been seeing that look on Rita's face for months now.

"Rita gave you this?" he asks.

"Yes. She wants you to have it. And I'm not taking it back." Sydney chuckles and kisses him.

Dante's jaw is clenched tightly as he wraps his arms around Sydney. He rests his head on her shoulder and cries as he remembers the woman, he called "Mrs. V."

He's been blaming himself since the day she died. This is the first time that he's allowed himself to actually grieve for her.

Rita unlocks the door to her and Keith's medical office. Although now, it's just hers. She had given herself two months to grieve, but now she has to get back to work.

She feels a thick heaviness as she walks into the office and flips on the lights. Somehow, everything looks different now.

She pictures herself and Keith running around the office, hanging up pictures and organizing supplies before they opened this place a few years ago. She never expected that she'd ever be running the office alone.

"Good morning," a soft voice says to her.

Rita turns to see her assistant, Trish standing in the doorway. She looks at Rita with sadness in her eyes.

Rita has grown to hate that look. Since Keith died, every person she sees looks at her with a deep sadness in their eyes and it makes her soul ache.

She remembers giving that look to other people in the past, trying to show them how much she loved them and how sorry she was for their loss. She never realized that somehow that look could cause more sorrow than it comforts.

"Hey, Trish," Rita says as she walks over and hugs her. Trish squeezes Rita tightly.

"I missed your controlling ass." Trish laughs with tears in her eyes.

"And I missed your nosey ass." Rita smiles and squeezes her again.

"How have you been?" Trish asks in a light tone.

"I'm exactly how you would expect me to be. Just pushing on, getting through every day." Rita shrugs with a half-smile.

"I'd expect nothing less from you. Your strength always inspired me. I know it hasn't been easy for you these last few years," Trish says.

"I used to think I was strong too. Now I don't know if I'm as strong as people think I am or if I'm just a really good actress," Rita says as she rubs her belly. She gazes around the room.

Trish looks at her with wide eyes.

"I'm trying this new thing where I actually say how I feel. I'm tired of wearing a mask. I've been doing that my whole life. I pretend I'm fine. I pretend my life is perfect, but it's not. I'm sick of pretending. It costs too much. If I had fought harder to get Keith some help instead of fighting so hard to keep his secrets, he might still be here," Rita replies.

"Wow, that's pretty deep. I can't say I agree with you about Keith though. I think you did everything you could for him." Trish waves her hand dismissively.

"No, trust me. There is a lot you don't know about him," Rita argues.

"Trust me, I know more than you think I do. Did you honestly think I didn't know he was using? I could tell every time he came in this office. I am a trained nurse, Rita. You tried as hard as you could to cover for him, but I knew he was on something. Damn, I probably covered for him as much as you did! And by the way, these walls are not as thick as you think they are. I heard you cussing him out in your office all the time." Trish chuckles.

Rita folds her arms as she laughs.

"Keith always said you were nosey as hell." Rita laughs.

Trish grins as she rolls her eyes, tucks her braids behind her ear, and clicks her tongue.

"I wouldn't call it nosey. I just pay attention," she says, still giggling.

"Well, I appreciate you paying attention...and having my back." Rita gives her a warm smile.

"Well, in the spirit of all of this honesty. The Feds did interview me about what was going on. They interrogated me, trying to see if you were involved in anything with Keith," Trish admits.

"Really?" Rita is stunned. She didn't know the staff had been brought into this. As if this hadn't been humiliating enough for her.

"Yes, they did. I want you to know that I did tell them that I believed Keith was using. I didn't tell them anything about him stealing the drug samples or treating patients while he was high. But I felt like I had to give them something, you know? They asked me about your involvement over and over, but I kept telling them you were innocent," Trish says as she looks Rita in the eye.

Rita lets out a sigh and nods her head.

"Thank you for telling me. I know you did what you had to do. Hell, I told them the same thing about Keith. He brought all of that on himself. You had to protect yourself. We both had to protect ourselves. You can't feel guilty for that." Rita hugs her.

"Ok, enough of this heavy stuff. How's my day looking?" Rita wipes away a single tear.

"Well, the rest of the staff will be here in a half-hour. Your first appointment isn't until 9. You have a light day today, Dr. Powers. I'll go get the office ready," Trish gives her a wink as she rushes off.

Dante sits in the apartment he shares with his mom and daughter. He's staring at the check Mrs. Virginia left him. He's had it a week and still can't bring himself to take it to the bank yet.

His mother almost fainted when he showed it to her. She slapped him when she found out that he's known about it for several months and never told her. She slapped him again once he told her he had initially refused to take the money.

Dante's mother, Barbara, walks into the living room where her son is sitting on the sofa seemingly in deep thought.

"Boy! You ain't put that damn money in the bank yet? You told me you would deposit it yesterday!" she says walking over to the couch and sitting next to him.

"I tried, Ma. I couldn't do it," Dante says solemnly.

"You gotta let yourself off the hook, baby. You're so busy punishing yourself, you can't even see when you been blessed!" she says putting one arm around him and pulling him close to her.

"When you told me you were going to be a father, I was terrified for you. I thought you were too young. You were twenty years old and I just knew you weren't ready for it. But I have watched you struggle and work to provide for that baby for five years. I have never been prouder of you in my life. I have watched the joy on your face when you were able to give her a good birthday and I've watched you cry when you couldn't afford to give her a nice Christmas." Barbara says, wiping a tear from Dante's face.

"What I'm trying to say is, God has given you a way to provide for your family. He's given you a way to make sure that little girl never wants for nothin'! You sittin' here throwin' it away! I know you loved Mrs. V, baby, everybody knows that. The only person punishing you, is YOU. But now you're punishing your daughter," Barbara says.

Dante sits up straight and uses one hand to wipe the tears from his face.

"I know you're right, Ma. But I don't think that's what's bothering me anymore. Mrs. V had this money for over a month before she died and didn't spend a dime of it. She always dreamed about winning the lottery and as soon as she did, she died, Ma," Dante says shaking his head.

"I feel like I need to do what she didn't get a chance to do. I mean, don't get me wrong, I am gonna take care of my family, but I feel like I also gotta think about what Mrs. V would be doing with her money if she was still here." Dante looks at his mother with sad eyes.

"That's beautiful, Son. I think she'd like that." Barbara kisses her son's cheek.

"Look, Ma, I know ya'll keep saying it wasn't my fault that she died. But in my mind, it was. So, I'm gon' buy you a house, set something aside for my daughter, but I'm not touching the rest of that money until I figure out how to honor Mrs. V." Dante stands up.

"I need you to come to the bank with me tomorrow. I don't know if I can do it by myself." Dante heads down the hallway and walks into to his bedroom shutting the door behind him.

The cool fall breeze blows through Sydney's hair as she, Sade and Tiffany crouch behind their car. They'll only have a few minutes to do this, so they wait as quietly as they can for everyone to get into position.

The night sky is clear. Sydney shivers as the breeze blows against her arms. She kicks herself for not wearing a jacket. She didn't want to cover her Black Lives Matter t-shirt that bears her mother's face.

All at once, about twenty other protesters rush over to them. They all wear t-shirts with Virginia's face.

Sydney, Sade and Tiffany leap up and run to the sidewalk in front of Officer Avery's home.

They won't have long since this is a residential area. As soon as their presence is known, the countdown is on until someone calls the police.

They begin chanting as loudly as they can.

"Her life mattered! Her life mattered!" They scream into the night.

Some hold posters showing Virginia's face. Others carry posters that call for Avery's arrest.

Officer Avery pokes his head out of his front door. He wears navy blue pajamas and slippers.
He walks out onto the porch and stands there. His feet glued to the ground. He doesn't speak. He just stares at them as his face turns beet red.

Neighbors walk outside as well. They stand and watch the protest. Some join in the chanting and grab signs. Others yell profanities and call for them to leave. They threaten to call the police.

Sydney and the rest have already planned to scatter before the cops show up.

To make sure no one gets arrested, they promised each other that no matter what, they won't stay longer than five minutes.

They wanted to make it clear to Officer Avery that him resigning from the force doesn't let him off the hook. They still want him to face charges for Virginia's death.

As Avery stands there unable to move. His wife peeks her head outside the door. She scowls at them, enraged by their presence.

She tries to pull her husband back inside the house, but he doesn't move. She jumps in front of him and pushes him inside and shoves him in the door. He stumbles over the threshold as he walks backward inside.

Once he's inside, she turns to face the crowd.

"You people get the fuck off our property! I'm calling the police! What more do you want from him? You already made him quit his job!" She screams red-faced.

Two teenage boys run outside of the house holding a carton of eggs. The two boys begin cursing and throwing eggs at the protesters.

Sydney glances at her phone and sees they've been there for seven minutes.

"Wrap it up! Let's go!" she shouts.

Officer Avery's wife grabs one of the eggs from her son and launches it into the crowd. It smashes into Sydney's face.

Sydney takes off running toward the red-headed, pale-skinned woman.

The crowd yells in chaos.

Sade and Tiffany try to catch Sydney and hold her back.

Sydney sprints quickly across the lawn and lands a punch across the woman's face who falls to the ground and howls in horror. She looks up at Sydney, who still has egg yolk dripping from her face.

Sydney wipes the yolk from her face and slings it at the woman as she stands over her. Sade grabs Sydney's arm and pulls her back toward the car.

Police sirens wail in the distance.

The sound snaps Sydney out of her rage.

She runs and jumps into the car. Tiffany hops in the driver's seat. The ladies speed away as the rest of the protesters disperse.

The next day, Sydney wipes down the counter after opening the store for the day.

"You punched her in the face? Seriously? That was stupid, Syd. You gotta be careful," Dante says as he places the cash register till inside the drawer.

"That bitch hit me in the face with a damn egg! That was self-defense!" Sydney says flippantly.

148

"Yea, self-defense," Dante scoffs.

"And what happens if they find out it was you, Syd? That's assault! Syd, you're going to jail!" Dante walks over to her.

His six-foot frame towers over her five-foot three build.

"Look at my eye! She hit me in my fucking eye! You expect me to just stand there?" Sydney points to her eye. Her light caramel skin is stained with a deep purple bruise circling her eye.

Dante grabs Sydney's face with both hands. He leans in and gently kisses her swollen eye.

"Baby, I'm just trying to look out for you. I know how it goes, somebody hits you, you hit back. That's how we were raised. But, after everything that happened with Jack, don't you think you should be a little more careful? The police are already watching you because of all this protesting you've been doing lately." Dante pulls her close to him.

"I know. You're right, baby. I'll be careful. But damn, it felt good to knock her ass out." Sydney laughs.

"I know it did." Dante chuckles with her.

The bell on the front door chimes as three white men in suits walk into the store.

Sydney recognizes one of them as the store owner. She's taken aback. He never comes in unless something is wrong.

"Mr. Gentry, thank you for coming down to meet with me." Dante trots over to him, shakes his hand.

"How about we set up in the back?" Dante ushers the men into the back room. As they head in the back room, Sydney grabs Dante.

"What's goin on?" She asks.

"I'm working on something. It's a surprise. I'll tell you later." Dante kisses her cheek as he heads to the back of the store and closes the door behind him.

Sydney eyes them suspiciously before heading back to the front of the store.

Rita is seated at her desk, finishing up her charting for the day. She groans as a sharp pain causes her to sit back in her chair. She closes her eyes as she pats her belly.

"I need you to calm down in there, little dude." She rubs her belly and smiles to herself. Trish taps on the door before walking in.

"You ok?" she asks noticing Rita's discomfort. She places a folder on Rita's desk.

"I'm good. I'd be better if you'd stop bringing me work so I can go home." Rita gives her a smile as she takes the folder.

She winces in pain again and takes deep breaths as she leans back in her seat.

"Are you sure you're ok? Those pains seem to be getting stronger," Trish asks.

Rita tries to answer, but another sharp pain takes her breath away.

"This has been going on for a few hours. Should I call your doctor?" Trish asks.

"No, I'm good. I've just been working a little too hard. I just need to go home and get some rest." Rita slowly stands up.

Rita heads over to the chair in the corner of her office to grab her jacket and purse.

"Dr. Powers!" Trish shouts as she sees a larger red stain on the back of Rita's khaki colored pants.

Trish rushes over and grabs Rita's arm.

"Dr. Powers, you're bleeding. I'm taking you to the hospital. You're ok, I got you," Trish says calmly as she tries not to show the panic she's feeling.

Rita hears nothing after Trish says she's bleeding. She knew something was wrong, but she didn't want to acknowledge it. She thought if she just kept going, it would all be ok. But she knew she was having contractions. She's only twenty-five weeks along.

She runs through the statistics of her baby surviving if he's born at five months. It's moments like this that make her hate being a doctor. Her mind always goes to numbers. She's forty-three. Her age makes this a high-risk pregnancy. The statistics say her baby only has about a fifty to sixty percent chance to survive life outside the womb this early.

Her body trembles as Trish rushes her out of the office. Trish tells the office secretary to lock up.

Rita can't speak. Trish is looking her in the eye and speaking to her, but Rita can't seem to make out what she's saying. She blinks slowly as she fights to catch her breath.

Suddenly, she feels hot. Her skin is clammy, and her knees are weak. Rita sinks to the ground as Trish tries her best to hold her up. Trish lays her on the ground, unable to lift her as Rita's body goes limp.

Rita watches as her staff gathers around her as she lies on the floor. She strains to catch her breath. The room goes dark as Rita loses consciousness.

Rita slowly opens her eyes. She blinks as she looks around the room. She quickly realizes that she's in a hospital bed.

She sees Sydney asleep in the chair next to her bed. Jack walks into the room sipping a can of soda.

"Welcome back, Ri Ri!" He smiles as he walks over and kisses her forehead. Sydney wakes up and stretches as she jumps to her feet. "You scared us, girl. How you feelin?" Sydney grabs her hand.

A single tear rolls from her eyes as she looks at her sister and brother.

"Is he ok?" Rita's voice croaks out as she motions to her belly.

Sydney places her hand on top of Rita's hand as it rests on her belly.

"I'm sorry, Sis. He's not in there..." Sydney says.

Rita tries to sit up.

"He's in the NICU," Sydney says quickly as she holds Rita down.

"He's ok, Ri. He's really, really small but he's ok. He's gonna have to stay in the NICU for a while, but he's ok." Sydney gently sweeps Rita's hair out of her face with her hand.

"Yea, he's good, Ri. He kinda looks like Dad," Jack says as he pulls out his cellphone and shows Rita a picture of her baby.

Rita's heart leaps in her chest as her eyes focus on the tiny person on the screen. He's the perfect combination of her father and Keith. Rita sinks back onto the bed as the tears flow. She's never been so in love with anyone in her life.

"I need to go see him. Take me to see him," she says to them without taking her eyes off of the photo.

Dante sits outside Mrs. Virginia's house waiting for Sydney. He called last night and told her he would pick her up for work this morning.

It's still early and the sun isn't up yet. Dante taps on the horn twice.

"I'm coming!" Sydney pokes her head out of the door and shouts.

A few moments later, she runs out of the house, pulling her jacket on one arm at a time as she jogs to the car.

"Sorry, I overslept. I guess I'm still not used to these early mornings," she says as she hops into the car and kisses his cheek.

She looks at the car's clock; it reads 4:45 am. They must open the store at 5:00 am.

"You good, Syd," Dante says as he speeds away from the house.

"At least you're only five minutes away."

Dante zips through the streets as quickly as he can. He whips into the gas station parking lot. Sydney notices the signs with the store logo are black.

"Damn! We forgot to leave the signs on again. I hope Gentry didn't drive by last night." Sydney hops out of the car and rushes to open the store's door.

"Syd, wait!" Dante calls to her as he runs to catch up with her. He stops her as she tries to unlock the door.

"I have a surprise for you. Stand here while I open the doors." Dante pulls Sydney out to the middle of the parking lot.

He opens the doors and goes inside. He turns on the L.E.D. signs that illuminate the store. Sydney's jaw drops.

The sign used to read "Stop and Shop" now reads "Virginia's Stop and Shop."

"How did you do this? Sydney gasps.

"Well, I'm the new owner. That's why I've been having all those meetings with Gentry." Dante brims with pride.

"It was your mother's favorite corner store. She stopped by almost every day after work. I wanted to do something to honor her," Dante says.

"I can't believe you did that." Sydney grabs him and wraps her arms around him tightly.

"Yea, and this just the first step. I'm negotiating to buy that abandoned school down the street. I think I want to open a community center. Your mother used to always tell me how much she loved this neighborhood and how much it hurt her to see how it's gotten run down over the years," Dante continues.

Sydney's mouth hangs open as he talks.

"I'm investing most of the money your mom left me in this neighborhood, Syd. I want to build a grocery store, a community center, a park. I want to see if I can help bring some jobs to this area and help keep some of these kids off the streets. I want ..." Sydney kisses Dante mid-sentence.

"I love you," she says as she looks into his eyes.

"You are such an amazing man. Now I know why she always talked about you the way she did." Sydney pulls him close and kisses him again.

"I'm in. I want to help. I think this is exactly what Mama would have wanted to do with her money." Sydney holds Dante's hand as they stare up at the sign bearing Virginia's name.

Jack pulls a large golden-brown turkey from the oven and sits it on top of the stove.

"Now that's a damn Turkey!" Jack boasts proudly.

"Boy don't get the big head! It ain't that hard to make a turkey! All you had to do was baste it and watch it cook!" Sydney cackles loudly, as she dances around the kitchen while "Before I Let Go" by Frankie Beverly and Maze blasts throughout Mrs. Virginia's house.

Sydney points over to the counter and brags about her homemade mac and cheese and her mother's famous dressing.

It's the first Thanksgiving since their mother passed away. Sydney is determined to follow all of her mother's recipes as closely as possible.

Jack promised to help her cook. He and Sydney always loved helping Virginia in the kitchen during the holidays. The smell of her dressing wafting through the house always smelled and felt like love.

Sydney desperately wants to feel her mother's love in the house today.

Rita dances into the kitchen holding baby Keith. He sleeps on her chest peacefully seeming to tune out the music and loud laughter.

He spent a month in the hospital. His doctor released him to go home a few days before Thanksgiving. Rita being a doctor herself eased a lot of concerns the doctor had about letting baby Keith go home.

Sydney rushes over and turns the music down when Rita comes in with the baby.

"You don't have to turn it down that low. This little guy needs to get used to how we do things around here. It ain't a holiday without music!" Rita laughs as she kisses the top of his head.

Sydney can't help but grin as she watches the pure joy on her sister's face. Having a child has definitely brought out a softer side of Rita.

Sydney puts an arm around Rita's shoulder and kisses her cheek.

"That's right, girl! You gotta train 'em early!" Sydney and Rita chuckle together.

"I guess I'll take this trash outside since Jack can't pry himself away from that damn turkey!" Sydney jabs at her brother.

Jack is still leaning over the stove fussing with his turkey.

"Girl, you can put a trash bag outside! Yo legs ain't broke!" Jack laughs as he bastes his turkey.

Sydney rolls her eyes and laughs as she gathers the trash and hauls it outside.

"What up, Syd!" Curtis calls to her from the sidewalk as he spots Sydney on the side of the house.

He's high. Sydney can tell by looking at him. Curtis is one of her neighborhood friends and used to be her supplier before she got clean.

Sydney waves nervously as Curtis approaches her.

"Damn you look good, girl! Where you been hidin?" Curtis says as he hugs her.

"Thank you. I've just been trying to stay out of trouble." Sydney steps back as his odor overwhelms her.

Curtis hears the music and laughter coming from the house. He smells the food coming from the kitchen.

"I ain't gon hold you, Syd. I see ya'll getting ready for Thanksgiving in there. I just wanted to stop and speak to you," Curtis says as he hugs her again.

Sydney holds her breath as he grabs her. His odor makes her eyes water. As he releases her, he grabs her hand and places a small plastic bag inside.

"You know I still got you if you need anything." Curtis winks at her as he turns to walk away.

Looking at the small bag of white powder in her hand terrifies her.

"Hey, Curt...look, I don't do that no more." Sydney forces the words out of her mouth.

Dante's car pulls up to the curb.

Sydney freezes as she holds the bag in her hand. She quickly stuffs it in her pocket.

Dante hops out of the car and trots over to Sydney. He eyes Curtis as he gives Dante an upward nod as he heads off down the street.

"What that nigga want?" Dante asks Sydney as he keeps his eyes on Curtis.

"He was just passing by when I took out the trash." Sydney shrugs.

Dante lets out a disapproving grunt.

"Look, don't be talking to that dude. He's still using Syd. You don't need that right now." Dante takes her hand and leads her to the side door of the house.

Dante slaps Sydney on her butt as she trots up the steps and into the house.

Dante stands there, unable to move as he watches a small plastic bag fall from Sydney's back pocket and land near his foot.

Dante picks it up. His heart breaks as he realizes what it is.

Sydney pokes her head out of the house once she sees Dante didn't follow her inside.

"Bae, you comin?" She smiles.

"This shit again, Syd? Again!?" Dante holds the bag up to her.

"I knew it! As soon as I saw that fool over here, I knew it!" Dante turns and stomps off toward his car.

Syd runs out and grabs him.

"Baby, I'm clean! I'm clean! He just gave it to me. I promise!" Sydney pleads.

"I'm supposed to believe that shit, Syd? Be honest! How long you been getting high? The whole time? Did you ever get clean?" Dante asks furiously.

Sydney steps back.

"That's not fair. Don't do that. I have been clean for months! You know that! You've been with me every day! Don't take away all the work I've done for one moment of weakness," Sydney shouts at him.

"I don't have to prove anything to you! Like I said, he saw me outside, and he came over here to speak. He gave it to me. I didn't ask him for it. I was trying to give it back to him, but when you pulled up, I got scared and stuffed it in my pocket. Cause I knew as soon as you saw it, you would start looking at me just like you're looking at me right now. Like I'm a damn crackhead." Sydney swats the tears away.

"I know you wanna leave. You can go." Sydney turns and walks back toward the house.

"I'm sorry, Syd," Dante says as he rushes to her.

He grabs her and pulls her close to him.

"You're right, I know you're better now. I've been with you every day. I see how hard you're working. Seeing that bag... it just scared me, I'm sorry." Dante kisses her hand.

Sydney nods her head as she wipes more tears away.

"Besides, I didn't come here for us to be fighting. I came here to be with my girl on Thanksgiving. No, actually I don't want you to be my girl. I want you to be my wife." Dante pulls a black box out of his pocket and slowly kneels on one knee.

Sydney feels as if the wind has been knocked out of her.

Dante opens the box displaying the amazing princess cut diamond.

"Sydney Marie Johnson, will you marry me?" Dante's brown eyes stare up at her waiting for her answer.

Sydney gently rubs his face with her hand. She kneels in front of him and softly kisses his lips.

"Yes." The word squeaks out as she wraps her arms around him.

Dante puts the ring on her finger and scoops her up in his arms. He carries her inside the house.

"We gettin' married, ya'll!" he shouts as he walks in.

Sydney bashfully covers her face as Dante sets her down.

"That's what I'm talking bout, bruh!" Jack shakes Dante's hand vigorously and pulls him in for a hug.

Rita hugs Sydney tightly.

"I'm so happy for you, Sis!" Rita says as she gushes over the gorgeous ring on Sydney's finger.

Later, they find themselves gathered around the dining room table. Their hearts are as full as their bellies as they laugh and eat.

They haven't smiled this hard since before Virginia passed. Eating a home-cooked meal with your family has a way of offering a sense of healing.

A knock on the door grabs their attention.

"That's probably Sheila, she had to go to her mom's house before she came over here." Jack eagerly hops up from the table and rushes to the door.

He throws the door open to find Officer Avery nervously pacing the front porch.

"You have got to be fucking kidding me, bruh! What the hell are you doing here? We are in here trying to have..." Jack stops mid-sentence as he sees Avery pull out a black gun tucked into the waist of his pants.

Jack can't move. He wants to run back inside, but he can't move. His feet are frozen in place.

Avery holds the gun with tears streaming down his face.

"I'm sorry." As Officer Avery utters the words, he holds up the gun and presses it to the right side of his head and without a thought, pulls the trigger.

Hearing the shot, Dante, Rita and Sydney run to the front door.

Jack is standing in the doorway. His eyes focused on the ground. He does not blink.

The group pulls the door open to find Avery lying on the porch, still and quiet. A sea of red surrounds him.

The group doesn't speak, nothing is left to say. It's finished.

In the end, Officer Avery felt he made it up to Ms. Virginia's family in the only way he could.

www.ingramcontent.com/pod-product-compliance
Lightning Source LLC
Chambersburg PA
CBHW020621250626
47154CB00004B/1606

ABOUT THE AUTHOR

Kimberly Kirby is an author, songwriter, and filmmaker from Memphis, TN. She's the author of the "Joy" book series and "What to do Until He Finds You". She has been nominated for Best Author in the Memphis Best in Black Awards.

In 2015 she wrote and directed her first short film, "Love Like This." Kimberly graduated from The University of Tennessee at Martin with a Bachelor of Science in Human Services.

Visit her website for more books: www.kimjkirby.com